THE DRIVE-THRU CREMATORIUM

JON BASSOFF

ERASERHEAD PRESS
PORTLAND, OREGON

ERASERHEAD PRESS
PO Box 10065
Portland, OR 97296

www.eraserheadpress.com
facebook/eraserheadpress

ISBN: 978-1-62105-280-7
Copyright © 2019 by Jon Bassoff
Cover copyright © 2019 Eraserhead Press

Printed in the USA.

PRAISE FOR THE DRIVE-THRU CREMATORIUM

"Jon Bassoff has written a stunning depiction of identity and isolation. He's doing something different here; *The Drive-Thru Crematorium* takes the surreal and the uncanny to new levels, well beyond what would deem the book Kafkaesque. Unlike Bassoff's protagonist, Stanley Maddox, who vanishes from the world at the beginning of the story, this book won't be erased from your memory anytime soon."

—Michael J. Seidlinger, author of *My Pet Serial Killer*

Throw the best of Richard Matheson, Ray Bradbury, Jim Thompson, and Charlie Kaufman in a blender and you might come up with something close to Jon Bassoff's *The Drive-Thru Crematorium*. It's menacing, unpredictable, and full of nightmares to shock us into a new reality. I finished it in one sitting and then went back out into the world, wondering if things would ever be the same.

—William Boyle, author of *Gravesend*

"In *The Drive-Thru Crematorium*, Jon Bassoff twines the mundane and the absurd together in a dizzying spirograph to produce an angst-ridden picture of modern society. Bassoff's novel is a shadowy feverdream in the best possible way—a story that both burns and chills and remains an unsettling thorn in the reader's psyche, longer after the last page is turned."

—Steph Post, author of *Miraculum*

"Jon Bassoff's *The Drive-Thru Crematorium* is a nightmarish feverdream of a novel that wrestles with the concept of identity and giving into our own worst impulses. Be spellbound by its twists and turns. Make sure you have a nightlight on hand when reading. Try not to scream as it races toward its frightening and shattering conclusion."

—Lee Matthew Goldberg, author of *The Mentor*

THE DRIVE-THRU
CREMATORIUM

I

STANLEY MADDOX

The happy ending is justly scorned as a misrepresentation; for the world, as we know it, as we have seen it, yields but one ending: death, disintegration, dismemberment, and the crucifixion of our heart with the passing of the forms which we have loved.

—Joseph Campbell, *The Hero with a Thousand Faces*

CHAPTER 1
A FORGOTTEN MAN

Stanley Maddox had worked at Evergreen Lending for six years before they forgot who he was.

It was a Wednesday, the last week of summer, and there hadn't been any issues on the Monday or Tuesday before (in fact, his boss had complimented him for his work on the McClusky loan and told him what a valued employee he was), but on this day when Stanley stepped out of the office elevator and zigzagged through the labyrinth of cubicles, copy machines, and filing cabinets, he could tell immediately that something wasn't right. It was the way the other workers looked at him with bemused expressions, the way they whispered to each other behind cupped hands. He heard one fellow, a short and bald man with a necktie hanging to his thighs, say, "Somebody needs to talk to him. But who? Don't ask me, I'm far too shy." At first, Stanley thought that there was an issue with his clothes, a tear in his pants perhaps, or maybe there was some food stuck in his teeth. Embarrassed, he quickly entered the men's room. He gazed at the mirror, turning this way and that, but he couldn't find anything amiss. And now he felt a sudden panic that he had done something illegal and/or immoral and would soon be arrested and perhaps tortured.

He washed his hands and wetted his face, forcing a smile to repress his anxiety. Exiting the bathroom, he strode to his cubicle and sat in his chair, the springs creaking beneath his weight. Dozens of files were stacked on his desk, including the McClusky loan on which he'd worked so hard over the last several days. Sighing deeply, he grabbed the file, opened it, and prepared to gather asset documentation. But every time he tried focusing on the numbers and signatures, he had the unsettling awareness of his coworkers staring at him with equal doses of suspicion and resentment. So for the next hour he merely stared at the paperwork and didn't check a single box, didn't validate a single number.

Not that he knew any of his coworkers all that well. He'd talked to a few of them on occasion—about the loans, about the weather, about the new Chili's Restaurant—but mostly he kept to himself, filling out forms and daydreaming about his next meal. Each day, when the clock struck five, he would quickly pack up and leave without saying goodbye to anybody. Despite the lack of meaningful social interaction, he'd never had any conflicts with any of his colleagues and had always been treated professionally and respectfully. Why, come to think about it, just the other day a big-boned woman who worked in the cubicle across from his had offered him homemade cookies and fudge. She smiled and said, "This will give you a little sugar high!" He took one of each and thanked her, and while he ate the desserts he felt very happy indeed.

By mid-morning, Stanley was finally able to refocus and ignore the sideways glances and whispers. Surely he was just being paranoid, he decided, an illness of thought birthed by a lifetime of news stories about terrorists, murderers, and rapists. As the fluorescent lights shone above him and the Muzak played softly behind him, Stanley neared completion of the McClusky loan and was looking forward to eating the turkey sandwich, pretzels, and chocolate pudding that he'd packed that morning. But then his boss, Mr. Elliot, approached him at his desk. He was a large man with a neatly-combed gray toupee, a timid face, and confused blue eyes. He wore a ruby ring on his pinky and a Timex watch on his wrist. He'd been with Evergreen Lending since its inception. For several moments, Mr. Elliot didn't say a word, just stood there gazing at Stanley. Not sure what was expected of him, Stanley pretended to work, flipping aimlessly through a file. Soon, Mr. Elliot cleared his throat, adjusted his hairpiece, and said, "Excuse me, but I don't think I caught your name."

Stanley's mouth opened and then closed again. He was understandably confused. After all, Mr. Elliot had been his boss for the entire six years of his employment. "I'm sorry?" Stanley managed to sputter. "My name?"

"Indeed. Are you the new underwriter? If so, you're not supposed to be here until next Monday. But I was told our new underwriter had green eyes. I've studied your eyes, and they are brown, like fudge. Almost black, actually. Like tar."

Stanley smiled, unsure if the old man was joking. "No, sir. I'm not the new underwriter. My name is Stanley Maddox. I've worked here for some time. Six years, in fact. I've sat in the same chair in the same cubicle. Why, just yesterday we spoke at length about the McClusky loan. You said I was an excellent employee."

Mr. Elliot stroked his chin and nodded his head. "Is that so? An excellent employee? I don't doubt any of that, Mr. Mallory, and I hesitate to call you a liar. Certainly, I am open to the possibility that it is my own weakness of mind that has caused me to forget one of my own employees. After all, I am not a young man, and in recent years I have shown some signs of mental deterioration. For example, I forget important dates, like my birthday. Was I born in March or April? Or was it September? And it is not unusual for me to get lost while driving a road I take every day. So, yes, forgetting an employee would fit into my pattern of forgetfulness. However, I have learned to compensate, and I am not so discourteous to call you a stranger to your face without discussing it first with my many employees. And that is exactly what I did. While you were working on completing the McClusky loan (by the way, did you verify his employment?), I asked several individuals in this office if they recognized you, and not one of them had. Is it possible that they too suffer from early onset Alzheimer's? Possible, but highly unlikely. To be fair, that lovely woman there" —and now he pointed to the woman who'd given him cookies and fudge— "feels that she may have seen you before, but she is quite certain that it was not here in the office. So you see, Mr. Mallory, it is more likely that it is your forgetfulness in this situation, and not mine."

"I see," Stanley said. He was surprised and saddened by Mr. Elliot's research but had to admit that the evidence was overwhelming and that it was pointless to argue with his deductions. Unless there was a conspiracy of forgetfulness, it seemed likely that it was he who was mistaken.

Mr. Elliot tapped on the desk with his knuckles. "Not to say you couldn't stay here, of course. We can always use the help. I see, Mr. Mallory, that you are quite adept at gathering the necessary information for our loans. We can certainly use your expertise and commitment. Unfortunately, I can't promise you any type of salary. You see, the interest rate being what it is, our margins are very tight. However, I don't think it's such a rotten deal to come to the office each day even if you aren't getting paid. At the very least, you'll have a roof over your head and tasks that will keep you busy and out of trouble. Our office is filled with kind and well-meaning people, and who knows? Perhaps one day something will open up for you. What do you say, Mr. Mallory?"

"It's Maddox," he quietly corrected.

"I apologize. Mr. *Maddox.*"

Stanley glanced around the office. Most of the workers had stopped what they were doing and were edging closer and closer to the conversation. He tried making eye contact with some of the familiar faces, but none of them showed any signs of recognition. He thought about the offer and had to admit that it was generous considering the circumstances. Indeed, there were other bosses who might have called the police and had him escorted out of the building.

"Yes," Stanley said. "I appreciate your words and I appreciate your offer. I'll continue to work hard, Mr. Elliot. And if the margins improve, perhaps I'll receive a portion of my salary."

"It's not out of the question," Mr. Elliot agreed. "Fine then. Feel free to remain at this particular desk, as I don't believe anybody else is using it. Let me know if you have questions about any of the processing jargon. And if you wouldn't mind, you can get started on the Russell loan. I believe it's right beneath Mr. McClusky's."

Stanley nodded his head. "Yes, sir, I will. Thank you, sir."

Mr. Elliot smiled and then nodded his head for such a long time that Stanley worried that he'd never stop. "Good luck, Mr. Mallory. And welcome aboard."

"Thank you, sir. It's good to be a part of the team."

And then Mr. Elliot walked away, and Stanley observed that the old man seemed to be lost, weaving confusedly through the office, mumbling to himself. When he was gone, Stanley looked around and noticed that many employees were still milling about, staring at him apprehensively. Ignoring them, he spread the Russell file open. He sighed deeply, rubbed his temples, and then got started on page one.

By the time five o'clock hit, Stanley was exhausted, his eyes burning and his temple throbbing. All of the other workers had left the office (had they made arrangements to leave early?) and it was just Stanley and an obese custodian. Stanley nodded at him and wished him a good night, but the custodian didn't respond, just dropped his head and pushed his broom across the linoleum floor.

Stanley left the building and hurried across the empty parking lot to his brown 2005 Buick Seville. He gripped the wheel and breathed deeply before turning on the engine. For the next twenty minutes, he drove aimlessly down the boulevard, past fast food restaurants, car dealerships, gas stations, and strip malls. And as he drove, he felt a sadness he couldn't name right away. Perhaps his anguish simply stemmed from the embarrassment of not being recognized at work. Or perhaps from the unexpected loss of salary. But, no. If he were really honest about things, he knew the real reason for his angst was the realization that a person could vanish from this world without anybody noticing or caring.

CHAPTER 2
THE RABBIT

The sky blackened, and Stanley finally came to his neighborhood, a freshly-built development full of streets with names like Meadow Lane, Sunbird Avenue, and Willow Way. All the houses were gray or beige and were identically structured with a long sloping driveway, a three-car garage, a small and tidy lawn, and a single skinny tree. Sterile and safe and silent. There were no cars parked in the streets and no people on the sidewalks. The curtains were all closed, the faint blue light of a television occasionally flickering behind them. Other than the number on the mailbox and the type of shrubs planted by the porch, there was almost no way to tell the difference between the houses. In fact, on more than one occasion Stanley had pulled into the wrong driveway and become frustrated when the garage door wouldn't open. It was okay, though. The nondescript architecture and neighborhood conformity comforted him. Provided a sense of camaraderie with the neighbors he rarely saw.

He parked in the garage, next to his wife's Honda Civic, and sat there for a long time with the engine on, staring through the dirt-streaked windshield at the blank wall in front of him, the man on the radio shouting about a blow-out sale at Sutter's Subaru. Maybe he would trade in his Buick. Subarus were reliable, he'd often heard, and reliability was his most prized attribute. Eventually, he clicked the engine off, grabbed his briefcase from the passenger side seat, and stepped into the garage, all neatly lined with gardening tools and potting soil and empty flower pots. The planning of a secret garden his wife would never create.

He opened the house door and shuffled through the laundry room and into the foyer. What a nice and comfortable house, he thought. When they'd first moved to the development, they'd been given the choice of three floor plans: Sanctuary, Presidential, and Sterling. They choose Sterling, and for that he was glad. It was just under 2,500 square feet of open floor plan with three bedrooms, a five-piece master bathroom, a main floor study, a spacious kitchen with granite countertops, and an unfinished basement. The furniture was Ikea. The decorations Pottery Barn. They were so happy.

Stanley dropped his briefcase on the floor and removed his jacket. His wife, Wendy, was sitting on the couch watching a movie on the Hallmark channel, something she did with increasing frequency. She didn't look up when Stanley entered, didn't look up when he approached her and placed his hand gently on her shoulder. "Hi, darling," he said. "How was your day?"

For a long time, she didn't answer. Then she turned her head slowly and said, "They finally delivered the deck chairs. Not more than two hours ago."

A nod of the head. "Well, that's good. Better late than never. And how do they look?"

"I like the style, but they're too dark. I wanted crimson not merlot. I'll have them exchanged, I think."

"Yes. I think you're right. Crimson would be better." He shifted his attention to the television. "What are you watching?"

Another long pause. "It's called *Devotion Comes Softly*. It shows how God can help you overcome any obstacle, no matter how big and impossible it might seem. You wouldn't like it. You have a hard time believing. That's what my mother always said."

"No. I might like it. I believe as much as the next guy."

Stanley watched the movie for a few moments, and he noticed that when the lead actress's eyes welled with tears, Wendy dabbed at her own. He cleared his throat. "Some strange happenings at work," he said. "Very strange indeed. Seems they've forgotten who I am. My boss. Everybody. My salary was eliminated, although they'll allow me to continue showing up each day. We'll have to make due, I suppose."

No answer from his wife. In the movie, the woman was bursting with emotion, a performance for the ages. Fists pressed against her chest, she whispered to her lover, "I… I have to stay for the right reasons. You know that."

The man (so very handsome!) pulled her close and kissed her. "I'll give you the best two reasons of all. Stay because I love you. And stay because God loves you!"

Violin music strained through the television speakers and Wendy was far gone, sobbing into her hands. Stanley knew that now wasn't the time to talk about lost wages, so he sighed deeply and lugged his way upstairs.

In the master bedroom, the queen-sized bed was neatly made and all the clothes were put away. The ceiling fan rotated, causing the tied-back curtains to sway gently. On the walls, there were pastoral paintings of lakes and trees and red barns. On the floor, soft cream-colored carpet. Stanley stood in the doorway and pulled his tie up over his head and began unbuttoning his shirt. But when he went to close the curtains he noticed a man in the house opposite, his face pressed against the dimly-lit window. He was banging on the glass and seemed to be yelling. Was he yelling for Stanley? Trying to get his attention? Was he in trouble? Was there a burglar or murderer in his house? Stanley felt paralyzed. He watched for some time and the man remained, his expression that of desperation, his face bright red. The police. He would call the police. He would let them know that a man was in trouble, his life perhaps in peril. But then, just like that, the man stopped shouting and pounding on the window. His face relaxed and he adjusted his tie and backed away slowly. Moments later, the light extinguished and he was gone.

Stanley rubbed his eyes and breathed deeply. Lack of sleep, it must have been. Senses frayed. His hands trembling, he managed to close the curtains and finish undressing. Then he walked to the bathroom and stepped in the shower. Turning the water to scalding, he thought about his job, and the screaming man, and his life, and he told himself that everything was fine.

Downstairs, the Hallmark movie was over, and Wendy was in the kitchen cooking steak and boiling potatoes. Stanley went to kiss her on the cheek, but she turned so he only got a piece of her ear.

"Smells good," he said. "I'm famished."

She nodded her head absently, wiped her hands on her apron, and flipped one steak and then the other. After leaning against the counter and tapping his foot for a few minutes, Stanley went into the dining room and sat down at the table. The candles were lit and everything looked lovely. He could hear Wendy whistling softly in the kitchen, and this was the American dream.

Eventually, she brought the food to the table, folded her apron on the chair, and sat down. Stanley thanked Jesus and the Heavenly Father and then they ate, the only sounds being silverware scraping on plates and mouths smacking open and shut. The food was good, although the meat was a bit overcooked and the potatoes in need of a coating of salt.

When Wendy finally spoke, her voice startled him. "There's a rabbit in our house," she said and then took a long sip from her glass of wine.

Stanley looked up, blinked a few times, and frowned. "A

rabbit you say?"

"Yes. A rabbit. With a bloody leg. I saw him earlier this evening. I chased after him with a broom, but he disappeared. His leg must have been gnawed by another animal. I had to scrub the carpet to remove the blood stains."

"Hmm. That's strange. Let me know if you see him again. I'll catch him. We can't have a rabbit in the house."

"A rabbit's foot is good luck," she said. "But not if it's bloody."

Stanley cut another chunk of steak and placed it in his mouth and then chewed very slowly. Wendy drank more wine and Stanley watched her from the corner of his eyes. She was pretty, although perhaps her eyes were a bit too far apart and her nose a bit too large. "And did you hear?" she asked. "Another woman was murdered right in her own house. Kayla Larson from the Meadowview neighborhood." When she said this, her voice seemed a bit too cheerful.

"Yes, I heard," he said, even though he hadn't. "It's a shame. How many is that now?"

"Six. In less than a year. I just can't figure out who would want to do such a thing. Killing just to kill. It must be some type of a demon, don't you think? Well, I guess the name they've given him—The Midnight Monster—is as good a name as any."

"Yes. I suppose it is. I hope they find him. I hope he burns."

And even though she hadn't eaten more than half her dinner, Wendy rose to her feet, wiped a wisp of hair from her face, and grabbed her plate from the table. "If you ask me," she said cheerily, moving toward the kitchen, "we all should burn. Every single one of us."

Stanley finished his dinner all alone. He slugged down his glass of wine and poured himself another one. Getting drunk was a decent option. But as he stared blankly at the wall, he saw something dart across the dining room floor.

The rabbit, leaving blood in its trail.

CHAPTER 3
THE CHANGING
PHOTOGRAPH

Stanley rose to his feet. He felt dizzy—maybe from the wine, maybe from the strangeness of the moment. He walked across the carpeted floor, eyes following the bloody prints. The trail led him through the sitting room and into the hallway. Occasionally, the prints would vanish, but then a few feet ahead would reappear.

"He's in here somewhere," Stanley said out loud. "I'll find him. He can't hide from his tracks."

The bloody paw prints circled around the hallway a few times and then Stanley noticed them on the stairs leading toward the basement. He breathed deeply and started down the steps. He wasn't exactly sure what he'd do when he found the rabbit. Grab it with his hands? Step on it with his foot? Capture it with a laundry basket? The basement door had been left open a crack, enough for the rabbit to squeeze through. Stanley followed after. Pitch darkness and so he had to fumble for the light switch. The fluorescent bulbs flickered on and his vision returned. The basement floor was bare concrete and the ceiling had exposed pipes and wiring. Cardboard boxes and plastic bins were stacked neatly against the wall. Wendy had labeled all of them: Christmas ornaments, extra blankets, giveaway clothes, etc. There were also several bookshelves, but instead of books they were stuffed full with antique dolls. How many dolls in all? Sixty? More? Wendy's mother had been a collector and had given them to her before she'd died (Virginia Slims/lung disease). Wendy didn't have the heart to throw them away, and now they sat on the shelves, the composition material cracking and peeling, the eye decals missing.

Stanley turned his gaze to the floor and saw more of the bloody paw prints, faint now, crisscrossing to the back of the basement where another door led to the furnace and water heater. The prints stopped there, but there was no rabbit. Confusion. Stanley spun around, trying to make sense of things, but there was no good explanation. The tracks only led to one place and it was the door, and the door was closed. And now he could swear that he heard one of the dolls giggle.

With unsteady hands, he pushed open the door and stepped into the furnace room. He hit the light switch, but it remained dark. Bad wiring. Mumbling to himself, he reached up and tapped the light bulb and it flashed on. He could hear the furnace thumping, could smell the dampness of the floors. He looked around. No sign of the wounded rabbit. But something equally strange. In the middle of the room were piles of pinewood boards, surrounded by a handsaw, tape measure, hammer, and framing square. And behind the wood and tools were three caskets, one sized for an infant.

Stanley raced upstairs. He called out for his wife, but she didn't answer. He found her in the bathroom, staring at her face in the mirror. The water was running and was tinged with blood.

Stanley stood next to his wife. "I saw the rabbit," he said, and she turned her head slowly.

"Rabbit? What are you talking about?"

"The one with the bloody foot. The one you told me about."

"A rabbit? In our house?"

"Certainly. You told me about him. Only when I followed him downstairs, he seems to have magically escaped."

Her eyes widened. "It's frightening!"

"And something else. I found wood. Planks. Tools. And three coffins, including a small one, as if built for an infant. Do you know where they came from?"

She shook her head. "Coffins? No. I have no idea. Maybe that man…"

"Man? What man?"

But Wendy refused to say anything more. She turned off the sink and returned her gaze to the mirror.

That night, Stanley and Wendy lay in bed. Wendy flipped through the latest issue of Cosmopolitan Magazine ("Are You Wearing the Right Foundation?" "How I Faced My Fears and Wore My Natural Hair for A Week" "Everything You Need to Know Before You Buy Antiperspirant") while Stanley stared at the wall, his gaze occasionally shifting to a photograph of him and his wife, taken years ago, shortly after they'd been married. There weren't many photographs of them in the house. In fact, when he thought about it, this might have been the only one. Not that it bothered him. He knew what his wife looked like and didn't need a photograph to remind him. He didn't know why she'd chosen this particular photograph to display. She wore a long blue dress and a white Easter bonnet and held a bouquet of daisies. She was staring directly into the camera with a wide, white smile. Her skin was beautifully tanned and her makeup perfectly applied. Stanley, meanwhile, looked disheveled. He wore his usual work shirt and tie, but the tie was too short and the shirt was pulling from his pants. His hair was unkempt, and he was staring at his own shoes, which were untied. Now he tried remembering something about the day. Had they gone for a walk in the park? Had they spent the morning searching for new drapes for the living room? Had they sat in church listening to a sermon on the importance of loving thy enemy? He couldn't recall a thing. But then again, remembering had never been his strong suit.

Eventually, Wendy closed her magazine, placed it on the nightstand, and turned off the light. She rolled on her side, back toward Stanley, and was soon snoring softly. That's the way it was with her. But Stanley couldn't sleep. His eyes remained open, and he saw and heard strange things that he knew weren't there: the rabbit gnawing off his own foot; Mr. Elliot, his boss, dangling from a noose; his neighbor pounding on his window, torso lit on fire; and the Midnight Monster whispering in his ear, "Don't worry, old fellow. The world will soon be taken care of my way. Blow out the fire before it burns you."

He tried waking Wendy, because he was scared, but she was a sound sleeper and didn't stir. Or perhaps she was faking slumber. Eleven o'clock, midnight, one o'clock, and finally Stanley drifted to sleep, dreaming of a world distorted and slanted. Strange creatures appeared and disappeared in his consciousness, and he tossed and turned and lashed at the mattress and his wife. He awoke at 6:28, two minutes before the alarm would have rung. Wendy still slept, her chest and shoulders rising and falling softly with each breath she took.

He lay in bed for some time and turned toward the window, gazing at the dull gray sky, raindrops gently pelting the pane. He felt sad and incomplete and wished he had the courage to make a real change in his life. Once again he looked at the photograph of him and his wife, but somehow it looked different than the night before. It bothered him and it took a long time to figure out the dissimilarity. While the poses and expressions of Stanley and Wendy remained the same, while the background was identical, he could now see that the cropping of the photo was different. Both he and his wife had shifted ever-so-slightly to the left, and now a portion of Stanley's leg and shoulder was gone from the frame. The world was a strange place, and he wondered how this transformation had happened in the middle of the night when everybody slept.

Stanley ate breakfast at the kitchen table. Corn Flakes and yogurt. A glass of orange juice. What he ate every morning (although on weekends, Wendy cooked them eggs and bacon and hash browns). He flipped open the newspaper. An enormous headline greeted him: "The Midnight Monster Strikes Again." Beneath the headline was a photograph of several police officers huddled with their heads down, obviously at a loss for reasonable theories.

And then the article itself:

Forest Grove – In this small suburban community men and women continue to be murdered, throats slit, in their own homes. Chief Officer Andy King calls this a "disturbing" trend, and says that "it is most likely the work of the same deranged individual—the Midnight Monster." King believes the murderer somehow possessed easy access to each of the houses he entered since there were no signs of forced entry. However, he would not comment on any possible connections between the numerous families who have been victimized.

The latest victim is Kayla Larson. Her husband, Frank, called his wife "an angel that God lay in our midst" and believes her murder to be "the work of the devil."

Six people have been murdered this year alone, including two in the last three weeks.

"Right now, we don't have much to go on," said Detective Elliot Benson, who is heading up the investigation for the Forest Grove Police Department. "We are asking anyone who may have information they think is relevant, no matter how small or seemingly trivial, to please call our anonymous hotline."

Police have been actively interviewing neighbors, business owners, as well as relatives of the Larson family. "All of us have the same motivation: the capture of the monster in our midst, and all of our energies are focused in that direction," Detective Benson told reporters.

Stanley refolded the newspaper and left it on the kitchen table. He felt sad about the victims but couldn't help thinking about the Midnight Monster, how he'd managed to terrify a community and what it must feel like knowing that your actions affected other people so quickly and powerfully.

He rinsed out his dishes and placed them in the dishwasher. Then he returned to the bedroom to get dressed. As his wife slept, he pulled on his khaki pants and buttoned his white dress shirt. He went to the bathroom and brushed his teeth and then went to work on tying his tie. Three tries before he got it to the right length. He sighed and studied his face in the mirror. Hair graying at the temples. Wrinkles developing around his brown eyes. And then he looked closer. Just below his cheekbone, he noticed a small flap of skin, the size and shape of a canine tooth. He took another step forward, so that his face was just inches from the mirror. Grimacing, he touched the flap with his finger and lifted it. The wound was deep and angry red, and looked as if it might be infected. "Who did this to me?" he whispered. Then a new thought popped into his head. What if this was just the beginning? What if the skin continued peeling, bit by bit, until his entire face was gone, leaving a monstrous one beneath? What would happen then?

CHAPTER 4
THE FIRING OF
STANLEY MADDOX

Band-Aid stuck to his face, Stanley walked through the lobby of Evergreen Lending, gripping the handle of his briefcase with both hands so that it bounced off his knees with every step he took. He got on the elevator with two people he recognized from his office. One of them was a woman with long, curly black hair and an enormous rear end. Her name was Shannon, or maybe Sally. The other was a young man with pasty skin and thick caterpillar eyebrows. Stanley didn't know his name. The entire time in the elevator, they both stared at him, seeming never to blink. Stanley tried ignoring them and watched the number above the doors change from two to three to four. As the elevator bounced to a stop, the woman leaned over, grabbed his arm and said, "Why are you here?"

"Excuse me?"

"Why are you here?" she said again in a tone that wasn't altogether unkind. "At this office? In this world?"

The doors opened and Stanley pulled away from her grasp and

stepped into the office. The woman and the man followed after him and every few seconds the woman said, "Why are you here?"

Stanley quickened his pace, but then a few of the other workers chimed in or, at the very least, nodded their heads in agreement. Stanley passed by his toupee-wearing boss who waved his hand and said, "Welcome back. Mr. Mallory, right?"

"Maddox."

"Apologies. As I said, some difficulty with my memory…"

He continued walking, doing his best to ignore the workers' taunts, until he came to the worker's lounge where he removed his lunch bag from his briefcase and placed it in the refrigerator. Then he walked toward his cubicle, located in the corner of the office near the women's restroom. But when he got there, he noticed that the cubicle had been completely removed. Someone had disconnected the partitions, and now instead of his workspace there was only a potted Ficus tree and a commercial water cooler.

Confused, he glanced around. He noticed that his files, the McClusky, Russell, and Sampson loans, were all stuffed in a wastebasket near where his desk used to be. And he'd worked so hard on them. Perhaps they'd been thrown away by mistake, he told himself. Resigned to his new reality, he bent down and removed the files from the trashcan, wiping off used Kleenexes and stale cake. Then he sat cross-legged on the floor, spread out the Russell file on his lap, and got to work.

All morning long people stepped over him, laughing and shaking heads, sometimes accidentally/on-purpose kicking the papers across the floor. But each time, he would simply get on his hands and knees, gather the papers, and continue his work. By eleven o'clock he'd finished the Russell loan and got started on the Sampson one. He kept himself motivated by thinking about lunch and that first taste of his sandwich.

Noon, and he closed the files and hid them beneath the Ficus plant so nobody would throw them away again. He went to the bathroom and took a dehydrated yellow piss and then washed his hands. He stared at the mirror and then yanked back the Band-Aid to check on his wound. It hadn't gotten any redder or angrier, but if he wasn't mistaken it had become larger, by just a millimeter or less. He'd have to keep his eye on it…

He exited the bathroom and went to the lounge. A half-dozen or so workers were sitting at tables already eating lunch. They talked about amortizations, escrows, and the Midnight Monster, but they became hushed when Stanley entered. He nodded his head, mumbled a "good afternoon," and walked toward the refrigerator, his stomach grumbling in anticipation. But when he opened the refrigerator door, he didn't see the lunch bag that he'd packed that morning. He moved aside bottles of soda and containers of mayonnaise and mustard, but his lunch was nowhere to be found. Had he forgotten to place it in the refrigerator? Had he left it on his counter at home? No, he clearly remembered placing it in the refrigerator, right next to a jar of Greek olives. As he stood there with the refrigerator door open, he heard a few snickers behind him. He glanced back and saw that a couple of the workers were watching him, pointing at him, and laughing.

And then he noticed something else. Sitting at the far table was an older woman, her gray hair strangled in a tight bun. Her lunch was spread out in front of her, and it consisted of a tuna sandwich, Lay's Potato Chips, Granny Smith apple, and a Diet Coke—the very lunch that Stanley had packed for himself. She looked at Stanley and her mouth tugged upward into a little grin. Stanley didn't know what to say or what to do, so he just stood there staring at her. More laughter from the other workers. "Can I help you with something?" she finally asked.

He rocked back and forth and buried his hands in his pockets. "I believe," he said, "that you have my lunch."

She looked at the food in front of her and then reached into the bag of Lay's and placed a chip in her mouth. She chewed slowly and returned her gaze to Stanley, but she didn't say a word.

"I'm sure it was an innocent mistake," he said. "Perhaps

you grabbed the wrong bag by accident."

Then her expression turned nasty and she took to imitating him in a mocking tone: *"I'm sure it was an innocent mistake."*

The other workers laughed some more and the old woman ate another chip and then another. Then, in the ultimate display of disrespect, she took his tuna sandwich and licked the top piece of bread from corner to corner. Stanley felt the blood coursing through his veins, felt his body trembling with rage. He tried remaining calm, tried remaining above the fray. When he spoke, he attempted to sound calm and unruffled, but the words that came out instead sounded pathetic.

"It's my lunch," he said. "I'll be too hungry. It's not fair."

A bite of the Granny apple. And then the sandwich. A long swallow of Diet Coke. And then she belched loudly and blew toward Stanley.

It was too much. He took a step forward and then another one. He felt his skin pulsing and wondered if his wound was still spreading. "It's not fair," he said again.

But before he could get any closer, several of the men and a masculine-looking woman rose from chairs and charged at Stanley. They were on him in a moment. One of them pinned his arms behind his back. Another one shoved his forearm against his throat. And a third tackled his legs, causing him to slam against the floor.

The old woman stood over him, gripping his Granny Smith apple. "How dare you threaten me," she said.

"I didn't threaten you," he tried to say, but his throat was constricted by one of the men.

For a long time, Stanley remained on his back, pinned to the floor. He tried to struggle free, but it was no use—he just wasn't strong enough.

"You walk in here like you own the place," the old woman said, and still Stanley couldn't respond.

How much time passed—ten minutes? twenty?—before Mr. Elliot entered the room. His tie was loosened and his shirt was untucked from his pants as if he'd been summoned from the restroom. He observed the fracas and said, "What in God's name is happening here?"

Stanley tried speaking, but the man's forearm remained pressed against his throat and his mouth was beginning to fill with blood.

Instead, a short man with hair combed straight down his forehead rose from his seat and began to explain the situation. "We were sitting here eating lunch like we always do, minding our own business, when this man, Mr...."

"Mallory," Mr. Elliot said.

"When Mr. Mallory entered and began threatening Susan here."

"Threatening?"

"That's right. Called her an old hag. Demanded that she give him her lunch. And when she refused, he threatened to gobble her up."

Mr. Elliot seemed stunned, shaking his head and massaging his sagging jowls. "Gobble her up? Mr. Mallory, is this true?"

Stanley managed to cough, but could muster no words

"This is most disappointing," Mr. Elliot said. "Especially after I went out of my way to allow you to continue working at Evergreen Lending. Well, that's what you get for putting yourself out for other people. Jesus was wrong, I'm afraid. I think it would be best, Mr. Mallory, if you left the property. Please leave on your own or I will be forced to have you escorted out. We can't have this type of behavior shown at my business. It won't do. It won't do at all."

And now some of the men, as well as the masculine woman, loosened their grip on Stanley and he was able to move to a sitting position. The man who'd been pressing his forearm against his throat pulled back, and Stanley gasped for breath. He spat out a mouthful of blood on the linoleum floor. Mr. Elliot stomped his foot in frustration.

"And who will clean up the floors, I ask you? Do you have an answer for that? It would serve you well, Mr. Mallory, to learn some manners. It would serve you very well."

Stanley nodded his head. His throat was throbbing, but he managed to speak in a raspy voice. "My last name is Maddox. And I'm sorry about your floor."

They did escort Stanley out of the building because there was mistrust that he might threaten the old woman again and perhaps even try to gobble her up. In the elevator the men talked about grills and hardwood floors and interest rates. Stanley could feel the blood filling his mouth again but forced himself to swallow it down.

They walked him through the lobby and had just shoved him out the front door and wiped their hands clean when Mr. Elliot came rushing outside.

"Mr. Mallory!" he called. "Mr. Mallory, please wait."

Stanley stopped and turned around. Mr. Elliot was jogging toward him and waving a manila envelope.

"What is it?" Stanley said.

"If it isn't too much trouble, I was hoping you might finish underwriting the Sampson loan. You won't be able to do it at the office, of course, but perhaps you can work on it from home. Normally, I wouldn't ask you to do this, but we are short staffed and so things are difficult right now."

Stanley stared at the old man, but he was too exhausted to feel enraged. He nodded his head slowly and grabbed the file from Mr. Elliot's hand.

"I'll have it completed by tomorrow morning," he said.

"Oh, good. That's wonderful to hear. You're a real credit to your race, Mr. Mallory. Indeed you are."

CHAPTER 5
THE DRIVE-THRU
CREMATORIUM

After he was escorted from the office, Stanley decided not to go home right away because Wendy wasn't expecting him for many hours and there was the chance that she was doing something he wouldn't want to know about. Instead, as was tradition, he went to the mall to buy some candy. He parked where he always parked, in front of the Olive Garden restaurant, and entered the front doors of the mall, the name Crossroads Shopping painted above a red, white, and blue star logo. He strode through the food court, past whining kids and agitated parents waiting in line for Chick-Fil-A, Sbarro, and Orange Julius, and toward Hammond's Candy Shop.

He grabbed a plastic bag and the metal scoop and picked his candies, the bright rainbow colors in contrast to the black ink and white paper of his job. Then he spent twenty minutes or so wandering through the mall, sucking his Tootsie pop and munching on his jellybeans, gazing at the displays behind glass windows, the high-styled mannequins gazing back at him.

Feeling happy (or maybe just experiencing a sugar high?) he returned to the parking lot and got back into his car and drove. Up and down Fillmore Avenue, packed with stores like Wal-Mart, McDonald's, Subway, Starbucks, Walgreens, Dollar Tree, Taco Bell, CVS, and Target. The new American West.

He'd just passed a car dealership with a thirty-foot American flag whipping in the wind, when he noticed a long line of cars entering a strip mall parking lot. There must have been twenty of them at least, all moving in the same direction. Was there some sort of an incredible sale? Or perhaps a celebrity sighting? Or a brutal car accident? Curiosity, so he turned on his blinker and followed the SUV ahead of him.

But as soon as he turned into the parking lot, he was forced to stop. A traffic jam. He glanced in his rearview mirror and there were already a half-dozen cars behind him. Even if he'd wanted to return to the avenue, there was no way for him to get there. He'd have to wait. The sun hung stoically in the sky, clouds coming apart at the seams. He turned on the radio and hummed along to a Michael Bolton song. *How Am I Supposed to Live Without You?* Every few minutes the cars edged forward.

It was twenty or thirty minutes before he could finally get a glimpse at what everybody was lined up for. In the far corner of the strip mall, right next to an abandoned electronics store, was a business he'd never noticed before, the sign flashing in pink and white neon: *Lifebridge Drive-Thru Mortuary and Crematorium.*

He felt bile in his throat and swallowed it down. A song by Kenny G. and then Celine Dion, and finally Stanley reached a narrow drive-thru lane marked with angels painted on the asphalt. Another four cars remained in front of him, and so he listened to Engelbert Humperdinck and Peter Cetera. Up ahead was a yellow gate arm, like the ones you would see in parking garages, preventing movement until the car in front was finished. Each car remained for about three minutes before moving forward and allowing the next car to enter past the opened gate.

Finally, it was Stanley's turn. He wasn't sure what to expect.

The gate opened and he edged forward. On the driver's side window there was a glass partition that was covered by a black curtain. There was also a slot for cards and money and a button that opened the register box. Stanley pressed the button and the metal door slid upward and allowed him access to the register. The man's name was Robert Vielle. He flipped through the pages and read the heartfelt inscriptions from friends and family: "Now you sit on the lap of our Lord," "Peace from the Baxter family; Jesus loves your soul," "A wonderful man taken from us."

Stanley had no idea what to write because he didn't know the deceased. He grabbed the pen and wrote the only thing he could think of, a biblical quote: "For dust you are and to dust you will return." And then, "I'm sorry you died."

He placed the register back in the box and pressed the button again and it closed. And now the black curtains opened and there appeared an elaborate wooden casket resting on a silver stand. On either side of the casket were floor lamps, and standing behind the casket was a tall and thin old man wearing a black suit, a gray tie, and white gloves.

As he gazed at the casket and then the mortician, Stanley felt uneasy. It was something in the man's rigid expression, something in his plastered gray hair, something in his pallid skin; Stanley couldn't take his eyes off of him. The man nodded somberly at Stanley, but there was a hint of cruelness in his eyes. With hands graceful and practiced, he lifted the lid of the coffin and now Stanley could see the formaldehyde-preserved man inside, mouth sewn shut, makeup slathered over skin. He looked to be about forty years old, balding and overweight. He looked like any of the employees at Evergreen Lending. He looked like Stanley himself.

Stanley stared at death for a couple of minutes, not sure if he should pretend to cry, and then he nodded at the mortician, whose mouth twitched into a vile smile before the casket closed and the black curtains followed. Stanley remained there for another minute, feeling lightheaded and agitated. Then he heard a horn honking, and he moved the car forward and out of the drive-thru lane.

Despite the strangeness of the wake, despite the strangeness of the mortician, Stanley found himself morbidly fascinated. And as he drove away, he decided that he would come back tomorrow and the day after that to see who else lay dead behind the curtain.

Early evening and the sun was lowering below the suburban asphalt and emptying parking lots. Stanley pulled into his neighborhood, barely noticing the black pickup truck loaded with heavy tools and machinery parked across the street from his house. He drove in the driveway, the garage door opening and swallowing him up.

He stepped out of the car and went inside. As usual, he could hear the sounds from the television playing the latest Hallmark movie. A woman's voice: "Just look at me! My hair is a mess. My lipstick is smeared. And I just can't stop crying."

The man: "Shh, shh. I don't care about any of that. To me, you're perfect."

As always, Stanley dropped his briefcase on the floor and removed his jacket. A deep sigh and he walked into the living room and gazed at the television where the man and woman were kissing and crying and laughing. Then he looked to the couch where Wendy sat.

And he was surprised to see a man sitting next to her.

CHAPTER 6
STRANGER IN THE HOUSE

The man was burly and strong and had a thick red beard. He wore work boots, jeans, and a flannel shirt. There appeared to be a wad of tobacco pressed between his lower lip and teeth, and Stanley noticed a scar spreading from the corner of his eye and disappearing beneath the beard.

For a long time, Stanley didn't say a word. He just stood there, rocking back and forth, trying to make sense of things. Was this stranger a relative of Wendy's? Somebody who'd come to repair the air conditioner? The man glanced at Stanley with indifference and then back at the television screen. For her part, Wendy watched the movie with rapt attention.

Finally, Stanley cleared his throat and spoke. "Hello. My name is Stanley. This is my house. I'm Wendy's husband."

The man again looked his way and then spit a stream of tobacco into a cup that was pressed between his legs. He didn't return the greeting.

"I don't believe I know you," Stanley said. "Are you a friend of Wendy's? A relative?"

The man blinked a few times and then shrugged his shoulders. "Jeff," was all he said. And that was as far as the conversation went.

Wendy, meanwhile, didn't seem to notice Stanley's presence, so engaged was she in her movie. Feeling anxious, he touched his finger to his Band-Aid and then to the skin below. He could tell that the wound had now crept below the edge of the dressing. "I'll get a glass of water," he said out loud. "I haven't had a thing to drink all day." Feeling a bit unsteady on his feet, he left the living room and went to the kitchen. His hands were trembling as he filled up the glass and pressed it to his lips, causing much of the water to spill on his shirt. He leaned against the sink and pulled back his thinning hair with his hand.

"When you've got somebody who loves you, the rest doesn't matter," echoed the woman's voice on the television.

Stanley stared at the clock, tick-tocking above the kitchen table. Impulsively, he reached into a drawer and pulled out a paring knife. Just in case. The man, Jeff, might be dangerous, and Stanley wanted to be able to protect himself. He untucked his shirt, placed the knife beneath his pants, and then re-tucked the shirt. Then he returned to the living room where the movie had just finished and the credits were rolling. Music was playing and Wendy, always sensitive, was crying. The man, Jeff, didn't try comforting her, but Stanley noticed that his right hand was resting on her upper thigh.

Stanley sat down on a chair opposite of them. The paring knife dug into his skin, forcing him to adjust his position. The television screen went black and Jeff grabbed the remote control and turned it off. Other than Wendy's soft sobs, the room was quiet.

"Today was another difficult day," Stanley said. "There was a misunderstanding at work. They don't want me to come back. It's not fair, but that's the way of the world. Nothing ever happens the way it should. A lot of people commit suicide. I won't do that, though. I believe in the Father, the Son, and the

Holy Spirit."

Wendy nodded her head slightly. Jeff rubbed her leg, his fingers nearly reaching her crotch.

Stanley continued. "Do you know what the morticians do with bodies after death? They use eye caps to keep the eyeballs round. They thread a needle around the jaws to keep the mouths closed. They drain the blood and replace it with embalming fluid. All to make the dead bodies look natural. Perhaps cremation is preferable…"

And now Wendy turned and faced her husband as Jeff continued maneuvering his hand. Her eyes narrowed and her face reddened. "And how, may I ask, are we going to live if you no longer have steady work? Do you expect me to live a life of poverty? Like Baby Doe Tabor? Is that what you expect?"

"No, no, of course not. I'll figure something out. Most likely, Mr. Elliot will change his mind. And if not, there are other ways to make money. Selling vacuum cleaners, for example."

She sighed and rested her head on Jeff's strong shoulder while his hand continued its ascent northward. "My mother was right," she said.

"About what?"

"About you."

Stanley didn't know how to respond. He'd never had any issues with Wendy's mother, and he'd always assumed she didn't have any issues with him. In fact, just last month she'd given him a new tie and a pair of dress socks as well as a card that said, "Happy birthday to a special son-in-law." But, then, he supposed Wendy had the right to be frustrated. Somebody needed to pay the bills. His loss of employment was an unwelcome development, that much was sure.

"Beer," Jeff said suddenly, and rose to his feet and disappeared into the kitchen.

Once he was gone, Wendy leaned forward and said, "Something else you should know. The rabbit is back. I saw it this morning. You need to take care of it. We can't be having a wounded rabbit running around our house, leaving trails of blood wherever it goes."

"No. You're right. I'll find it. And I'll kill it with my bare hands. Break its neck. But who is this Jeff fellow? He seems like a nice man. And certainly very strong. I've never met him before, I don't believe."

But she only scowled and said, "It's none of your business. Why do you even care?"

"Well, you're my wife and this is my house and—"

"Ha! You don't know shit about your house, Stanley. You never have. Don't start pretending like you care now."

Well, maybe she was right. Stanley got up from the chair. "I'll do better," he said. "I'll figure out a way to make money. I'll find and kill the rabbit. Now, if you don't mind, I'll go upstairs and take a shower."

Just then, Jeff reappeared from the kitchen holding his beer as well as a plate of pickles. Stanley walked toward the staircase, and he could feel both of their eyes bearing down on him. He had a knife, and he could use it if the time was right…

Once upstairs and inside the bedroom, Stanley removed the knife from his pants and dropped it on the dresser. He went to close the curtains, worried that the screaming man from yesterday would be staring back at him, but thankfully the window was darkened and the man was nowhere to be found. He got undressed and hopped in the shower and stayed there for a long time, singing half-remembered songs, trying not to think about any of the strange events of the past few days.

When the hot water turned lukewarm, he stepped out of the shower. The Band-Aid had fallen from his face and he was scared of what the mirror would reveal. He remembered a story he had read as a child about a man whose appearance miraculously changed every day, forcing him to transform his personality as well. One day he was a rich white man, the next he was a black beggar. Stanley had liked the story because living an entire life as the same person is mundane and occasionally torturous. But now he wanted predictability. He used the side of his hand to wipe the steam from the mirror. Then he glanced sideways, keeping his eyes narrowed as if to protect himself from the upcoming image. The wound had indeed gotten worse. Whereas yesterday it was the size of a canine tooth, today it resembled the opening in a soda can, the skin flapping below.

The dead skin needed removal, of that he was sure. Stanley quickly retrieved the knife from the bedroom dresser and then returned to the bathroom. Teeth gritted, he lifted the knife to his face. Just a quick slice and then it would be taken care of. But his hands had never been steady, and as he maneuvered the blade toward his face, he jerked, accidentally puncturing the wound. Blood dripped down his cheek, and he cursed. He grabbed a wad of toilet paper, but even after pressing it to his face, the bleeding continued, soaking through the layers. He pulled more and more toilet paper from the roll, trying to get the bleeding to stop, but the wound was deep, and the bleeding continued. And now he noticed that other parts of his body were bleeding as well. His leg, where the knife had pressed when he sat down. His shoulder from an accident many weeks ago. His belly from a source unknown. And so forth. He did his best to move from one wound to the next, placing pressure on the injury and then moving on to the next one. He began feeling lightheaded. Was it possible, he wondered, to bleed to death from a multitude of small cuts? He thought about shouting for Wendy or perhaps dialing 911 and declaring this a medical emergency, but that would mean admitting that he was weak, so he remained in the bathroom for another twenty minutes at least until he managed to get all of the blood to clot. Unnerved, his breathing and heart rate slowed. He located bandages and tape in the medicine cabinet and spent the next several minutes bandaging all of the gashes, crisscrossing a pair of Band-Aids across the wound on his face. "Maybe nobody will notice," he whispered. "Maybe the wounds will make me stronger."

Stanley combed his hair, got dressed, and limped downstairs.

He could smell dinner wafting from the kitchen. Pork chops and green beans and mashed potatoes. In the dining room, the candles were lit and the wine glasses were filled. But there were only two places set, and Wendy and Jeff were already seated, napkins on laps. Was this some type of a joke? He, who was now covered with wounds, was being denied dinner? For several minutes, Stanley stood at the head of the table, not speaking, only watching. He kept waiting for Wendy to apologize at her thoughtlessness and rush into the kitchen to get Stanley his dinner, but that didn't happen. Instead, Jeff mumbled a nonsensical grace and then the two of them started eating.

It was as if Wendy and Jeff were the ones who were married. Food was stuffed in mouths as Wendy talked of mundane things, as always, listing the housework she'd completed, the dress she intended to purchase, the crabgrass that needed to be cut. Jeff continually grunted some affirmation in response, and Wendy looked at him and smiled, a lovely expression smitten with desire.

Stanley was understandably furious. This time, the two of them had gone far too far. Acting as if *they* were the happily married couple. Still, he'd never been somebody who felt comfortable in confrontations, and he had no desire to make a scene, not tonight. So other than stomping his foot on the ground and whispering "So that's the way things are going to be," he kept his frustration to himself. Recognizing the fact that Wendy had no plans to feed him, he eventually returned to the kitchen and fixed himself a makeshift dinner: a peanut butter and jelly sandwich, some potato chips, and a couple of Oreo cookies. He returned to the dining room and dropped his plate on the table. Only two chairs, so he ate standing up, while Wendy and Jeff finished their home-cooked meals, oblivious or indifferent to Stanley's suffering.

Throughout the entire dinner, Wendy only acknowledged Stanley for a single moment: when she saw the Oreo cookies on his plate. She shook her head in disgust and asked him why he was eating them.

"Because I like Oreos," he said.

"I know you do. And that's why you're getting fatter and fatter. Is it any wonder that I can barely stand looking at you?"

Stanley took a small bite of the cookie and dropped it back on his plate. She was a cruel one, that was becoming plainly obvious.

"Now why don't you take care of the dishes," she said once they were finished eating. "Jeff and I are going to watch another movie."

The two of them rose from the table and left the dining room, Wendy placing her hand inside of his. Stanley didn't know how to react. He should have hit him, he supposed. Or maybe hit her. Instead, he got to work on the dishes, thinking violent and wicked thoughts all the while, knowing full well that he was too gentle to ever follow through on any of them.

CHAPTER 7
FATHER'S VOICE

That night, while Wendy and Jeff watched *The Love We Can't Forget* ("Please remember how it felt the first time we walked hand-in-hand down the shore"), Stanley stayed in the upstairs study and worked feverishly on processing the Sampson loan. He inputted data from Mr. Sampson's W-2 and 1099 forms as well as recent paychecks and last year's tax returns. He listed debts and assets and then cross-referenced names and numbers until he was confident that the loan was processed properly and ready to be delivered to the underwriter. He leaned back in his chair and daydreamed that Mr. Elliot would be so impressed with his work that he would allow him to return to the office and maybe even earn a paycheck. And once Stanley proved himself again and again through more impeccable loan work, Mr. Elliot would have no choice but to promote him to an underwriter or even an appraisal analyst. Then what would Wendy think about him? Then she would tell him how proud of him she was, how she always believed in him.

With great pride, he slipped the processed loan back in the folder and placed it on his desk. Tomorrow he would bring the folder, as well as a cup of steaming hot coffee, directly to Mr. Elliot and then everything would be different.

It was nearly midnight when he rose from his desk and turned off the office light. He went downstairs and drank a cup of warm milk and checked to make sure all the doors were locked (the Midnight Monster, remember). After so much stress and anxiety, he could feel his body begin to relax. He walked upstairs, pausing at the landing to yawn and stretch. A good night's sleep, and then sunny skies. But when he entered the bedroom, he was disappointed to find that Jeff was in bed with Wendy, his muscular arm wrapped around her slender waist. He should have expected it, of course, but it was still discouraging. After all, having a stranger replace you at the dinner table is one thing, but the bedroom is another thing entirely. On their wedding day, hadn't she vowed to be faithful? He would have to review the video from the ceremony to be sure. But, then again, he could hardly blame her. Over the last several months, he had been distant and distracted, so it only made sense for her to find comfort in somebody else's arms.

In addition to the philosophical quandaries, there was the pragmatic issue of where to sleep tonight. He was, after all, exhausted. He supposed he could curl up on the couch downstairs or in the guest bedroom, but that struck him as patently unfair. Indeed, this was his house, too. He'd paid for it with his hard-earned money. There was no reason for him to be banished from the bedroom just because his wife had taken a liking to some blue-collar worker. So instead, Stanley crawled in bed, trying to find a little space where he could comfortably sleep for the night. At first he squeezed in next to Jeff, one leg dangling off the bed, but then Jeff moaned and swung his arm backwards, connecting on the bridge of Stanley's nose.

He didn't know if the blow was intentional or not, but it was clear that there wasn't enough space for the three of them. He considered maneuvering into the limited bed space between Jeff and Wendy, but he was afraid he would awaken one or both of them and that could lead to a shouting match or, worse yet, a fist fight. He finally settled for curling up in the fetal position at the foot of the bed, the lump of Jeff's feet pressing against his thigh. He sighed deeply and closed his eyes. He knew that he would have to stay very still, that he wouldn't be able to flip over because of restlessness, but that wasn't too big of an issue in the grand scheme of things. He thought of all the homeless people in faraway cities forced to sleep in bus stations and street corners and decided that sleeping at the foot of the bed in his own beautiful house wasn't all that big of a sacrifice.

He soon fell asleep, forcing thoughts of gratitude.

But it wasn't long that his slumber was interrupted by his own anxiety, his eyelids popping open. He could hear Jeff snoring loudly, could hear Wendy laughing in her sleep. Jeff's foot was now pressing against Stanley's bladder, and he needed to pee. He tried pushing the foot away, but Jeff moaned, so Stanley let it be, not wanting to wake him without cause. He turned his head so that he was facing the footboard, and then his eyes jerked toward the wall. The moon shone through the gaps in the curtains, and he watched the shadows crawl across the walls and ceiling. Then his eyes rested on that photograph of him and Wendy, the one taken so many years ago on a long forgotten day. He blinked a few times, trying better to focus. And although it was dark, and although his senses couldn't be trusted, he was sure that the photograph had changed once again. He was sure that his figure had moved even farther out of the photograph. Whereas before, a portion of his leg and shoulder had been cropped out of the photo, now they were both gone completely, as well as maybe a quarter of his face, his left ear and eye vanished. While Jeff's foot dug into his bladder and stomach, while Wendy continued laughing, Stanley remained focused on the photograph and wondered who it was that was trying to drive him crazy.

Forty-five minutes, an hour, Stanley remained awake, afraid to move, eyes fixated on the photograph. That's when the phone rang, the jangling echoing against the walls. Stanley glanced at the clock—nearing two in the morning. For some reason, he wasn't surprised by the phone ringing. He was surprised, however, that neither of his bedmates awakened. The phone kept ringing. Five rings, ten, fifteen. Stanley pushed his way out from Jeff's foot and maneuvered until he was off the bed. Despite some moaning and groaning, Jeff and Wendy both remained asleep. The phone kept ringing.

Stanley tiptoed across the carpeted floor and left the bedroom. He made his way through the hallway and down the stairs. He'd reached the living room and was about to pick up the receiver when the ringing stopped. Stanley stared at the phone in disgust. From outside he could hear cats fighting and shrieking.

He had just turned around and taken a step away when the phone rang again. Clearing his throat, Stanley grabbed the receiver and placed it to his ear. "Hello?" he said. On the other side of the receiver came only the sound of heavy, labored breathing. "Hello?" Stanley said again. "Who is this? What do you want?"

More breathing. No words. Stanley hung up the phone, but seconds later the ringing started again.

Skin becoming hot with rage, Stanley picked up the receiver and said in a raised voice, "Stop this nonsense or I'll call the police."

But now on the other end, he could hear a voice, weak and barely audible. "Stanley? Is that you? Stanley?"

A voice from so long ago.

"Father?"

"Yes. Yes. It is your father. Stanley. It's been such a long time."

Stanley glanced around to see if anybody had been woken, but his shadow was the only one. "Father. I'm sorry. I meant to come and see you. Things have been hectic at home and at the office."

"I understand…"

"You see, I got a new promotion. Assistant manager. More money, but more responsibilities."

"I always knew you had it in you, son."

"And Wendy and I are looking forward to starting our own family. She's pregnant, you see. We're hoping for a boy, but as long as the baby is healthy…"

Stanley didn't know why he was lying, but he felt compelled to do so. His father began hacking and coughing for several long moments causing Stanley to worry that he would die.

"Father, are you okay? Father?"

Eventually the coughing stopped and the old man spoke again, although his voice sounded ragged and weak.

"It's such a shame," he said. "Such a terrible shame. I must be cursed."

"What do you mean?"

"You with a wonderful new job. Wendy expecting a beautiful baby."

"Yes. How are you cursed, Father?"

"I don't have long to live, son. Not long at all. A few days at the most. A few hours, possibly. Consumption, they say. Tuberculosis. My immune system isn't working properly. It's a terrible way to go, son. So painful."

"A few hours? I… I'm sorry. I'm so sorry."

And now Stanley felt angry at himself for being so self-centered. Here he was focused on the loss of his job, the loss of his wife, the Midnight Monster, while his father was slowly dying. But then, that was silly. He hadn't known his father was sick. How could he have? His father never called. Their relationship had long since soured.

"I will come and see you, Father! Before it's too late. I'll come right now. It will take me an hour to get to your little town, and then another fifteen minutes to locate your house near the train tracks. Is there anything I can bring? Are they treating you fine? Hold tight, Father, please."

On the other end of the line there was more coughing. "I look forward to seeing you, Stanley. I will be here, huddled in my blankets, waiting for your arrival."

Stanley hung up the phone and then hurried up the stairs. He got dressed in the moonlight while Wendy and Jeff slept, his wife still giggling at unknown dreams. He didn't want her to worry about him if she woke and found him gone, so he located a piece of stationary and wrote down a quick note: "My father, Alan Maddox, is dying. I have gone to sit with him and comfort him. I will be back in the morning. I will take the trash out then."

He placed the note on the dresser where he was sure she'd see it. He was about to leave the room when he noticed that the window curtain had somehow been pulled back. He walked across the room to close it and for the second time saw the man in the dimly-lit house pounding on the window, pleading for help.

CHAPTER 8
A DEATH IN THE FAMILY

His father lived in Bellwood in the same house that Stanley had grown up in. It was usually an hour drive from Forest Grove, but at this time of night, without any traffic, Stanley was able to make better time. Down the highway he drove, away from chain stores and shopping malls and cookie cutter developments, his headlights cutting through the fearsome darkness. He listened to talk radio and it was filled with shrill voices warning of the apocalyptic country we were bound to live in, vote this way or else. The voices eventually turned to static, but Stanley left the radio on because noise was better than his own thoughts. He gripped the steering wheel tightly and wiped perspiration from his forehead. Not another car on the highway and he worried that he might be dead without knowing it.

By the time he finally arrived in Bellwood, it was past four in the morning and the sky was filled with dead stars and a quarter moon. Down Harrison Avenue, turn right on 7th Street, and then left on Pine. The house was a big Victorian, once proud and select, now crumbling and rotting. Stanley parked his car and stepped outside, pulling up his collar and sucking in the cold air. He walked across the dirt yard and took the stairs slowly, his left knee throbbing from an injury he couldn't remember. There was music from somewhere far away and laughter from even farther. He knocked on the door but nobody answered, so he tried the handle and it was unlocked. Stepping inside, he saw that everything was distorted and slanted, a German expressionistic painting.

He walked up the stairs and down a narrow hallway, paint peeling, moldings cracked. Doors to bedrooms were all closed, but not his father's room. For a moment, he was a child again, terrified of facing the old man and his booming voice and disapproving eyes. And now he stood in the doorway, frowning, terrified once again. A deep breath, and he stepped into the room. He thought he heard whispers, but, no. The window was closed and his haggard image stared back at him, the wound spreading by the second. Floorboards creaking beneath his feet, he walked toward the bed where his father's body and face were covered by layers of blankets.

There was a chair next to the bed. Stanley sat down on the chair and watched his father sleep. But after observing for a few minutes, he noticed that the blankets were still, and he worried that he was too late and that his father had already died. "Father?" he said, voice in a panic.

No response.

"Father. It's Stanley. I've come to make amends. Can you hear me?"

Still nothing. Stanley pulled back the blanket. The old man's creased face was gray, and his jaw was slack. Stanley shook his shoulders and patted his cheeks, but there was no response. First the corpse at the Drive-Thru Crematorium, and now this. He rose from his chair and walked quickly through the hallway then took the stairs two at a time and raced into the living room. Unnerved, he located the phone that sat on an end table by the couch. He dialed 911 and told the operator his name and his emergency. "It's my father," he said. "He's not breathing. Tuberculosis, he has. I'm afraid he might be dead. I could always bring him to you, if it's too much trouble…"

But they told him to wait where he was, that they would be there shortly, and so he hung up the phone, sat on the couch, and buried his face in his hands. He thought about returning upstairs, but he couldn't bear to be in a room with a corpse, especially his father's. It wasn't long until he could hear the sirens echoing through the streets. They would be here soon enough and they would take away his father. And then he wondered about the will, about where his father wanted to be buried…

He got up from the couch and went into the kitchen. There was the same round, wooden table that had been there when he was a child. The same chairs and cabinets and curtains and refrigerator. Nothing had changed. He'd left a long time ago, but nothing had changed. He opened the refrigerator and grabbed a bottle of beer. He twisted it open and took a long swallow. His mother. How had she died? He couldn't remember. It was a long time ago, and memories were always changing. Cancer maybe.

He finished the beer and then drank another. The sirens continued moaning, but the ambulance didn't show. He could call them again. Find out what the delay was. Perhaps a wreck on the highway or perhaps the Midnight Monster had struck this town, too.

Five o'clock and then five-thirty, and still the ambulance didn't come. He thought about his wife and wondered if she'd seen his note and if she was worried about him. He thought about the Sampson loan and how he needed to hand deliver that to Mr. Elliot first thing in the morning. He thought about the man in the window and the wounded rabbit and the infant casket. He was thinking about all of those things when he heard footsteps creaking behind him. He turned around and was surprised to see his father.

***

The old man wore flannel pajamas, the bottom three buttons open, allowing his gut to burst through. He was an enormous and imposing man, and now his face had regained its color and he was very much alive. Outside, the sirens still moaned.

"Father!" Stanley said and rose to his feet, but in his surprised movement, he knocked over his bottle, the beer quickly spreading across the table. He grabbed paper towel and wiped up the liquid, all the while his father stood in the doorframe, his thick arms folded in front of his chest in disapproval.

When the table was dried, he turned and faced his father. The old man was silent, and Stanley felt the need to speak. "Father, listen to me. After our phone call, I got here as quickly as I could. I wanted to see you before your death."

But his father didn't answer, just took another step into the kitchen, his eyes narrowed and mean.

"When I came up to your room, I… I thought you were dead. Your face was gray. The covers weren't moving."

Still no words from his father. Feeling more and more anxious, Stanley returned to the refrigerator and grabbed another beer, the last one remaining. He drank it quickly, his stomach beginning to lurch. He leaned against the sink and looked at his father. "I called for an ambulance. They should be here soon. Don't you hear the sirens? How are you feeling? How can I help you?"

Still nothing.

"Father, Father. Why don't you speak? Please. I came all this way to check on you. I thought you were dead. Please. Say something."

His father now smiled, but there was no warmth in the smile. "Your mother is of no concern to you," the old man said. "She was never of any concern to you. And now you dare to show your face. After you betrayed me. After you abandoned me. While the tuberculosis got worse and worse. The coughing fits. The chest pain. The exhaustion. You find out who cares for you in times of trouble. Not you. Not you."

Stanley felt the blood drain from his face. "I'm here now, Father. I left in the middle of the night and drove a long way. I am your only son and I want to—"

"Not my only son!" the old man boomed. "Not a son at all!"

Stanley didn't know what had gotten into his father. It must have been the illness affecting his thought process. He needed to remain calm and not become defensive.

"I'm sorry that you're upset. I have tried to be a good son. I work hard and have a wonderful wife. And now she's pregnant. Now you'll be a grandfather. I drove a long way to comfort you. I'm still your son."

"Liar! All lies! Not a word of truth coming from your mouth."

There was knocking at the front door. It must have been the paramedics finally arriving. Stanley moved toward the knocking, but his father blocked his way.

"It's the emergency workers," Stanley said. "I'll let them in and they can look at you. Make sure you don't need to go to the hospital. It wasn't so long ago, I thought you were dead. You should get checked out."

"Sit down," his father growled. "I'm not through with you."

"But, Father."

"Sit down!"

And so he did.

The old man moved forward so that he was standing directly over his son. His face was red and his eyes were bloodshot. His cheeks and nose were covered with broken blood vessels.

"When you were a baby, I pierced your ankles and left you on the mountainside. Do you remember?"

"Father?"

"If only you'd died!"

"You're not well. That's the problem."

"A betrayer!" the old man shouted. "That's what you are."

"That's not fair. You can't say that I—"

"The riddle of the Sphinx, Stanley! The riddle of the Sphinx!"

And now the front door slammed open and a trio of paramedics rushed in. As soon as the old man heard them approaching, he fell to his knees and then to his stomach. He began convulsing, white foam oozing from his mouth.

One of the paramedics, a young man with a crew-cut, approached the seizing body and turned him on his back. A female paramedic asked, "What happened to him? How long has he been sick?"

"I don't know, exactly. He was dead, and then he was resurrected. But he only returned to condemn me for my sins."

The old man was trying to speak, but his mouth was filled with foam, and he couldn't stop convulsing. The paramedics held him down and shot him with medicine and for a moment the seizing stopped, and he managed to pull himself up enough to point at Stanley. "He's my betrayer," he said. "He's my killer."

The paramedics all turned and looked at Stanley who began backing out of the kitchen.

"The riddle of the Sphinx!" he said again. "The poor woman hung herself, and it was all because of him. And now me. My death on his hands as well!"

Stanley pushed his way out of the kitchen and raced toward the front door. As he glanced back, he saw that the paramedics were all still staring at him and that his father was dead.

He stepped outside and he could hardly breathe. The sun had risen and the sky was filled with blood. And as he raced down the steps, he saw the memory of his mother, and she was dangling from a twisted tree. For several long moments he remained, his father dead inside, his mother dead outside. And then he thought of the Sampson loan which needed to be delivered to Mr. Elliot, and he rushed to his car.

CHAPTER 9
THE BIRTH

It was nearing eight in the morning by the time Stanley arrived home. He called for his wife, but there was no answer. The television was on, but Wendy wasn't there to watch it. A lonely laugh track echoed against the walls. No sign of Jeff either, and for that he was glad.

He walked up the stairs, and now he was sure he heard the sound of Wendy singing softly. He reached the second-floor landing and her voice became clearer. He recognized the song from another lifetime. A song his dead mother used to sing to him:

Each night I'm lonely by the fireside
Alone with an aching heart
As I held in my arms
The dearest of charms
Just a little old rag doll

The door to the bathroom was opened a crack and Stanley could see Wendy lying in the bathtub, lathering her long legs with soap. He stood there for a minute, hoping she wouldn't notice him. But it wasn't long before she smiled and said, "Well, are you just going to stand there watching me?"

Stanley backed up a step. "I... I'm sorry, darling. I didn't mean to make you feel uncomfortable. I just arrived home."

"Yes. It must have been a long night. And how's your father?"

Stanley shook his head and stared at the floor. "Unfortunately, he passed this morning. Complications from tuberculosis. I'm glad I got to see him before he died. I'm glad I got to make peace. And then there was my mother. She hung herself, years ago, and I had forgotten. These things are always difficult."

For several moments, Wendy didn't speak, as if she were trying to make sense of his words. Then she placed her head under the water, and Stanley worried she was trying to drown herself. But, no, she was just rinsing the shampoo from her hair. Soon her head reappeared and she wiped the water from her eyes. "It's too bad they died," she said. "Death is always such a drag." A long pause, and then: "I know you must be terribly sad, but when you get a chance, could you please take out the trash? It's beginning to smell, and we could get maggots."

"Yes," he said. "I will do that now. And where's Jeff?"

"He's at work," she said. "At the stockyard."

He took one last look at his wife, trying his best to ignore the feelings of lust. Then he went downstairs and pulled the trash from the kitchen and brought it to the dumpster in the garage. He emptied the dishwasher and reloaded it, and then he cleaned the counters and swept the floors. Certainly, he would prove himself as a worthy husband.

When he returned upstairs, Wendy was out of the bath and standing in the bedroom, a towel wrapped loosely around her body. Stanley entered, keeping his head down and his gaze averted. But he couldn't help notice when the towel dropped to the floor. He raised his head and gazed foolishly. Her hair was long and yellow, and her eyes were as vacant as a china doll. Her skin glistened from the bath, nipples erect on full breasts. He wanted to embrace her. He wanted to strangle her. It was a peculiar feeling, and he felt ashamed.

And now Wendy started laughing. "Look at you," she said. "Like a poor little puppy. I know what you want, darling. But why are you so bashful?"

Stanley took a step forward and then another one. Wendy continued to mock him.

"It's just that you know what Jeff has been doing to me. Every day when you're away at work. And that makes you feel mad. But now you're home, and Jeff is nowhere to be found. He can't hurt you now. Come on, Stanley. Come to Mommy."

He kept moving forward, and now Wendy backed up a step, but her smile remained. It seemed that the floor was moving and that he'd never reach her. But then her back was to the wall and he was standing directly in front of her, his skin pulsing with desire. He reached out and pulled her toward him. She didn't resist. He kissed her, his tongue pushing inside of her mouth. He felt the blood rushing in his veins. Separating from her, he quickly removed his shirt, pants, and boxers.

He wanted her, wanted to ravage her perfect skin and her china doll face, but now she stood in the corner, hand covering her mouth, shoulders bouncing up and down. At first, Stanley thought she was crying and he was going to comfort her, but he quickly realized that she was laughing, always laughing. She removed her hand from her mouth and shook her head and pointed at Stanley, toward his midsection. Horrified, he looked down and regarded his own penis, shriveled, the size of a white button mushroom.

"I'm sorry," she said through giggles. "Sometimes I just can't help myself."

At this, Stanley sat down on the bed and placed his head in his hands. And then he began sobbing. He knew it was pathetic, but he couldn't help himself. Tears rolling down his cheeks, moans emanating from his throat, he cried for all the small defeats and humiliations that made up his life. He wished so badly that he could be someone else, that he could be empowered, feared even. But no, he was stuck with himself, forgettable, impotent, and static.

For some time, his wife watched him, still giggling, but then she stopped and sat down next to him and, in something resembling empathy, placed her hand on his shoulder. "It's okay, Stanley," she said. "Don't cry. It's not so bad."

But he couldn't stop. The tears just kept coming. Wendy remained with him on the bed for a while, saying words of encouragement and patting his leg, but eventually she became bored and rose to her feet. She walked across the room and began getting dressed.

But she had just finished buttoning her floral dress when she shrieked.

Stanley's head jerked upward. "What?" he said. "Wendy, what is it?"

She pointed at the floor, beneath the bed. "The rabbit. It's under there."

"Under the bed? Are you sure?"

She nodded her head slowly. "I saw it move. It's hiding in the corner. You need to get it. You need to kill it."

You need to kill it.

He wiped the tears from his eyes and got to his feet. He was still naked and felt self-conscious.

"I should put my clothes on first," he said.

And so he grabbed his boxers and his pants and his shirt and got dressed while Wendy backed against the wall, her finger still pointing beneath the bed, her face stretched into a grimace of terror.

"Hurry," she said. "It's bound to escape."

Stanley looked at his wife and then at the bed. He wasn't sure what to do. He'd never caught a rabbit before and was a little frightened. But he immediately got upset at himself for feeling that way. It was a rabbit, for Christ sakes! What could he possibly be afraid of?

"Hurry," Wendy said again.

Stanley got down on his hands and knees and peered under

the bed. Other than Jeff's blue jeans, he didn't see a thing.

"It's not there," he said. "You must be imagining things."

"No," she said. "It's there. I'm positive. Look again. It's probably up against the corner. I won't be able to sleep until you find it. I won't be able to sleep until you kill it."

Once again he peered beneath the bed, and once again he didn't see anything. He was about to get to his feet when he saw a quick movement from the corner of his eye. He blinked a few times. Now he was sure he saw a pair of eyes shining from the shadows.

"Yes," he said. "I think I see it."

On his knees, he swiped a few times, but his reach wasn't long enough.

"Go close the door," he said. "In case it tries to escape."

Wendy followed his orders and shut the door, leaned against it. Stanley got on his stomach. Head turned to the side, he reached one arm under the bed and grasped blindly. He came up empty. Frustrated, he shifted his body position and tried again.

"Get it," she said. "Kill it."

But without being able to see what he was reaching for, it was difficult. Once again he peered beneath the bed. Once again, he saw the eyes shining. One more swipe and this time his fingers touched something soft and warm. He squeezed his hand shut and jerked the rabbit from beneath the bed.

But when he looked down, Stanley saw that it wasn't a rabbit at all. It was a baby boy, his body slicked with blood.

CHAPTER 10
THE RADIO SERMON

Stanley immediately released the baby's leg and toppled backward. He looked at his hand which was now covered with blood and quickly wiped it on his pants. When he glanced behind him, he noticed that the door was open and Wendy was gone. Typical. The baby was crying, screaming really, its eyes closed and its body shaking. Stanley moved slowly toward the creature. He reached onto the bed and yanked off the top sheet and then spread it on the ground. Not sure what else to do, he dragged the baby onto the sheet and worked on cleaning him, but his effort was ineffective—the blood had dried on his skin. The creature cried louder, with more agony, and Stanley worried that he was wounded.

He didn't know the proper way to hold a baby, so he gripped him at his rib cage, his own arms outstretched. The baby's head lolled back and forth, and he continued shrieking as Stanley brought him across the hallway to the bathroom. "Wendy!" he called out. "Wendy!" Nothing. With one hand he pressed the crying baby against his chest, and with the other hand he turned on the bathwater. He made sure the water was lukewarm, and once it reached a few inches in height, he gently placed the baby in the tub and watched as he slid on his back, flapped his arms frantically, and cried even louder. Stanley used a soapy washcloth to clean the blood off his body, scrubbing particularly hard on his face, and then removed him from the tub and wrapped him in a towel. Still, the baby was angry as hell.

As he walked into the hallway, the baby stopped crying for a moment and buried his face in Stanley's shoulder. But it was no gesture of affection as Stanley now noticed a greenish-black tar-like substance smeared onto his own chest. Cursing under his breath, Stanley quickly returned to the bathroom and used the bloody washcloth to clean up the mess. And he'd almost finished that task, when the baby rewarded him with a warm flow of piss on his neck and face. Bubbling with rage, Stanley quickly turned the baby the other way so that the piss sprayed on the sink and mirror. "Wendy!" he called, desperately. "Wendy!"

Without any diapers, Stanley was forced to get creative. He grabbed a pillowcase from the hallway closet and used a scissor to cut a pair of holes in the bottom. The baby was nearly swallowed up by the pillowcase, so he cut and trimmed until the top of the makeshift diaper only reached the bottom of his rib cage. He used a stapler to tighten the diaper, and by the time he was finished, perspiration was forming on his forehead, but the baby had finally stopped crying.

"There, there," he said. "Good, baby."

Stanley glanced at his watch. It was nearly ten. He remembered the Sampson loan, the one he'd promised he'd return first thing in the morning. Now it was already mid-morning, and he was still at home trying to care for a baby. He felt like he'd let down Mr. Elliot and would never be able to earn his trust again. And more frustrating was the fact that this baby most likely wasn't even his. It couldn't be. Early in their marriage, he and Wendy had tried to conceive without any luck. They'd gone to fertility clinic after fertility clinic and it was determined that Stanley was sterile. But who, then, was the father? Was it Jeff? Or were there more furtive visitors to his house?

He couldn't help feeling angry and resentful. It was now clear that Wendy had hidden the baby from him, pretending, for some reason, that it was a rabbit. Well, he couldn't be expected to continue caring for the baby, especially when he had business to take care of at work. In the meantime, he would find a place for the baby to be safe. Perhaps he would leave him in the bedroom with the door closed or, better yet, in the drained bathtub where the little creature couldn't get into any trouble at all.

But he'd only just placed the baby in the bathtub and shushed away the tears when Wendy reappeared. She wore a blue floral maternity dress with fake pearls hanging around her neck.

"Oh, Jesus," she said, eyes widening. "What the hell are you doing, Stanley?"

"This was the safest place I could think of, you see. I need to go to work. Mr. Elliot is expecting the Sampson loan. I couldn't find you, so I—"

"It's just like you!" she shouted. "Placing our little Ian in the bathtub. What's wrong with you? The poor thing needs his mommy. He's probably starving."

Ian. The baby's name was Ian. He hated that name.

Feeling ashamed at his actions, Stanley bent down and pulled Baby Ian from the bathtub. He handed him to Wendy who immediately pulled her left breast from her dress and pressed the baby's mouth against her nipple. The baby sucked ravenously, his hands grabbing at his mother's skin, his eyes glaring at Stanley suspiciously.

"It's good that you're feeding him. I hadn't thought of that. And I'm hardly equipped."

"Just go," she said. "Leave us be. The baby and I are bonding. We don't need you to get in the way."

"Yes. Of course. I'll be going to work, then. And on the

way home, do you need me to pick up anything at the store?"

"Diapers," she said. "And beer for Jeff."

"I'll write it down so I don't forget. I shouldn't be at the office for too long." Then he watched his wife feeding the boy and for a quick moment he felt full of love and joy. "It's really quite wonderful, don't you think? Our own little family. Father and mother and son."

But she just laughed and shook her head. "Go to work," she said. "We'll be fine without you."

"Yes," Stanley said. "I know you will be."

Stanley wore a pair of Band-Aids on his face, but as he drove to work he kept pulling them off and studying the wound in the rearview mirror. "A monster," he whispered to himself. And then the voice of a radio talk show host: "A monster. Or, to be specific, the Midnight Monster. In his bloody hands, our town is becoming a devastation. He slaughters the innocent when they sleep then races unseen through the suburban neighborhoods, the moon flickering through the blackened clouds. Beneath ground he lives, or perhaps in a shack filled with bones and shrunken heads, body parts preserved in jars of formaldehyde. Yes, a monster, and monsters do terrible things—like The Human Dracula, for example, who drank his victims' blood and ate their hands, or The Sorcerer who buried girls waist deep, or The Chessboard Killer who murdered men with a hammer before inserting a vodka bottle into their skulls."

The man's voice was southern and angry, and Stanley, for his part, was engrossed by the sermon, because he felt a strange kinship with the Midnight Monster, for reasons unclear.

"But don't you find it strange that none of the house members ever hear a sound? That none of them ever notice anything amiss? The police have gone from house to house, interviewing subjects, dusting for fingerprints, casting footprints, collecting hair, but there are no clues, nothing to break the case, and they've wasted an inordinate amount of time on individuals claiming to be the Midnight Monster himself, only to find that their stories were flimsy and they were merely lonely psychotics or attention whores. Like Harry 'Swordfish' Tempest who brought the police into his apartment to show him the heads he'd saved, only to reveal the heads were of the plastic variety, torn from his dead mother's kewpie dolls. Or Bill 'Shore Leave' Plunkett, who, in a fit of tears, handed them his confessional diary, written in dream-logic, detailing not only how he'd bled-out his victims, but also confessing to his role in the assassination of Archduke Ferdinand."

Stanley tapped the steering wheel with his fingers. Of course people were taking credit for the Midnight Monster's crimes. Of course they were.

"At the police station, they stick notes and photographs on the walls, crisscross strings on the town map, and write a list of suspects, which include not a single one. Because none of the families had any enemies, not in a safe and placid town like Forest Grove. A serious question for you: is this a human being laying waste to our community or is it something more terrifying? Don't scoff, people. You don't believe in the supernatural? Well then, I think you should start believing. Perhaps he enters through a crack in the window or the space beneath the door or maybe he never enters at all. An evil power beyond our understanding."

"But I understand," Stanley whispered.

A pause in his sermon, and Stanley worried the radio had gone off the air. When the preacher spoke again, his voice was barely louder than a whisper. "Oh, Lord, give us guidance. The streetlights and stop signs are the witnesses, but they remain mum, and how many times can we listen to the mournful cries echo from the dimly-lit bedrooms while The Midnight Monster gallops through the darkness?"

CHAPTER 11
THE CELEBRATION

Stanley arrived at Evergreen Lending and parked at the far end of the lot. He stepped out of the car and hurried toward the cold and sterile building, the paperwork for the Sampson loan safely inside his briefcase.

As he walked through the glass doors and into the empty lobby, he couldn't help but feel anxious. He was confident in the job he'd done on the Sampson loan, but Stanley recalled the recent ugly confrontation in the employee's lounge and worried about the reaction. Would the workers welcome him with open arms, thankful that he'd completed the all-important Sampson loan? Or would they attack him with verbal barbs and physical shoves, tear the loan from his hands and drag him back to the streets like some deranged vagrant? But he supposed there was no point in worrying. What was that old quote by that dead author? "People become attached to their burdens sometimes more than the burdens are attached to them." It was true. He needed to be reasonable. Life was too short. He thought of his poor father, white foam rising from his mouth, and then the baby Ian, body coated with blood. He would let his burdens go, fall like ash to the ground. He entered the elevator, pushed the floor button several times to be sure, and then closed his eyes as he floated upward.

When the doors opened at the third floor he saw that dozens of co-workers were gathered near the elevator, as if they'd been anxiously waiting for his arrival. Stanley considered huddling in the corner of the elevator in the hopes that nobody would notice him, but a fat woman whom he didn't recognize pointed at him and shrieked loudly.

Now the mob moved toward him, arms outstretched, and he feared they would crush him against the walls, breath gone forever. And his thoughts drifted to Giles Correy, the accused witch, who died between two large boards as more and weight was pressed on him all the while he shouted, "More weight, sirs! More weight!"

Stanley turned his back toward the mob and covered his head with his briefcase, gritting his teeth in preparation for the white-collar rampage, but he soon realized that they weren't after his blood.

"A cigar for the old lad!" came a voice, and when Stanley lowered his briefcase and looked up, he saw that it was Mr. Elliot, an Earl Grey-stained grin on his face, a pair of cheap Swisher Sweet cigars in his hand.

While Mr. Elliot held out his offering, a few of the other coworkers guided him from the elevator, all the while patting him on the back and saying things like, "Well done, my good man" and "A joyous day indeed."

Even the woman who stole his lunch was there to give him congratulations, leaning forward to kiss his cheek, the soft whiskers on her chin rubbing against his skin.

Soon the cigar jutted from his mouth and he choked as he sucked down the smoke.

"A cigar, Mr. Mallory. Don't inhale. It'll make you quite ill."

"Thank you, Mr. Elliot. And I'm Maddox, not Mallory."

"Apologies. Terribly sorry."

But Stanley was really touched by all the attention and well wishes. It seemed the entire office had stopped processing loans in order to celebrate Stanley's achievement—although what that achievement was he wasn't totally sure.

They led him through the office toward his cubicle, the partitions fully rebuilt, and on his desk were bouquets of flowers and envelopes containing cards. Pink and blue balloons floated throughout the office, and the fat woman who'd offered him cookies and fudge some months back carried a giant cake with the word "Congratulations" misspelled as "Congradulations." It really was something.

Chairs were soon brought out and a makeshift table was assembled for the cake as well as several liters of Mr. Pibb and Diet Rite soda.

As Stanley puffed on his cigar and accepted all the hugs and handshakes, he decided that it had been a long time since he'd felt this accepted and loved. And just to think that a couple of days earlier they had been escorting him out of the office for a crime that he hadn't committed, slandering his good name—although it was true that it was the wrong name (Mallory) that they'd been slandering, so perhaps it wasn't slander at all. But none of that mattered now; that was all in the past. If there was one thing you could say about Stanley it was that he had a tremendous amount of faith in mankind and, in particular, mankind's ability to evolve and right the wrongs of the past. He believed in redemption every bit as much as he believed in iniquity.

They served the cake and soda, and Stanley left his cigar burning on the table.

"C'mon, Mr. Mallory," said a bald man with a wispy mustache. "We can't eat until you take the first bite. Company tradition."

Stanley looked down at his plate and regarded the piece of cake, flakes of dark frosting falling on his plate, and for some reason he thought about ash, and he wondered, he wondered.

With more encouragement, Stanley finally scooped a piece

of cake with his plastic spoon and placed it in his mouth. He
let the dessert melt on his tongue and decided that it didn't
taste good at all. In fact, it tasted like what Stanley imagined
a dead person's flesh might taste like, and he had to focus very
hard not to gag or vomit. But the rest of the Evergreen workers
seemed to be enjoying the cake, which meant that most likely
they hadn't baked the corpse he'd seen at the Drive-Thru
Crematorium, ground-up teeth replacing the sugar, curdled
blood instead of whole milk.

He took another bite of the corpse cake and then grabbed
his cigar and took a puff of that, letting the smoke trickle
from the corner of his mouth. Music was playing—John Tesh,
who he'd always liked ever since the media personality left his
position as host of Entertainment Tonight to pursue his dream
of becoming an adult contemporary pianist, selling out shows
from Des Moines to Helsinki, a pretty major accomplishment
if you asked Stanley.

The cake was finished and the soda almost so, and now
they brought out presents, dozens and dozens of them, and Mr.
Elliot encouraged Stanley to sit on the floor, cross-legged ("just
like a little boy"), so he could open each and every one of them
while his coworkers cheered him on.

It seemed that every single person in the office had brought
him a gift, from the El Salvadorian custodian to Mr. Elliot
himself. Some, like the emphysemic sales rep, had even brought
him multiple gifts, so enthused were they by the celebration.
Stanley couldn't help but recall birthday parties from when
he was young, rooms filled with balloons and streamers and
screaming boys, but maybe he was confused, maybe those
parties hadn't been for him but instead for somebody he'd seen
on television or the movies. But certainly this made up for it.
This validated him as a Mortgage Loan Processor and as a man.

"Open my present first!" said a skinny woman with frizzy
hair and a badly chipped front tooth. She handed him a present
wrapped with today's newspaper and its gruesome headline:

"The Midnight Monster Strikes Again."

Nodding and mouthing "Thank you," Stanley crushed out his cigar on the sole of his battered shoe and took the present into his hands.

As his coworkers gathered around smiling and chattering excitedly, Stanley began tearing off the shiny paper, his heart beating rapidly. He opened the box and found inside a little baby onesie with the words "Daddy's Little Cutie" on it. And next to that, a wooden rattle decorated with cartoonish Indians in headdresses.

At first he didn't know what to make of it, but he still showed gratitude by smiling and saying, "Oh, thank you, thank you." But just a moment later he realized the significance of the gift, the significance of the festivity: they were celebrating the birth of his son, the one that Stanley had only discovered that very morning, at first thinking it was a bloody rabbit. This realization made Stanley feel very uncomfortable. After all, he was convinced that the baby was illegitimate, and it was embarrassing receiving all of the gifts and adulation for an accomplishment that wasn't his. However, as John Tesh blasted through the speakers, Stanley decided that it would be rude to call for an end to the party, one that had obviously taken many days, weeks even, to plan. So, despite his uneasiness, Stanley showed a happy face, opening present after present, each one containing another onesie or a bottle or a receiving blanket or wet wipes.

But after a while, after so many worthless presents and feigned thank yous, he couldn't take it anymore. Now he suddenly stood up, his feet buried in wrapping paper, and made his pronouncement. "I'm sorry," he said, struggling to make his voice heard. "These things are never easy to say, but I feel I must. I have some doubts as to whether I'm actually the father of the bloody boy. You see, ladies and gentlemen, I happen to be sterile."

For a long moment there was a hush, and to Stanley it was

deafening. He felt that, once again, he'd let everybody down, the way he had with his father and mother and wife.

"I'm sorry," said an old man with a block of a hearing aid, "but did you say you're sterile?"

"Yes. I'm afraid I did. My sperm count is a good deal lower than five million, which would make it nearly impossible for my wife to conceive."

And now there was a general murmuring, the lending professionals trying to decide how to deal with this latest development. Would they demand that he give the presents back? Would they attack him with the pent-up rage common to every paper pusher on earth? Or would they surprise him again and treat him with kindness and love?

After several minutes of discussion, some of it heated, most of it civil, Mr. Elliot stepped forward from the crowd. He cleared his throat and adjusted his toupee, although it remained askew on his head.

"We imagine that this must be very difficult for you, Mr. Mallory. Very difficult indeed. But you did the right thing. Sharing such private information was, frankly, quite courageous. And I think I speak for everybody at Evergreen Lending when I say that you will make a fine father, whether or not the baby is blood-related. Indeed, it is love and devotion that makes a man a father, not the machinations of God's DNA. So it is with great admiration and respect that we encourage you to open the final present, a gift that we all purchased together. We hope you will understand the symbolism and significance and will take it to heart."

Stanley was once again overcome with emotion. Such empathy! Such humanity! His eyes welled with tears and he was forced to wipe them away with his sleeve. It was one thing to be benevolent at a time of great accomplishment, but it was far more impressive to show empathy to somebody in their great sorrow, somebody like Stanley.

"I thank you," Stanley said, his voice quivering. "I thank

each and every one of you. From the bottom of my heart." But as he spoke, he realized that the tears from his eyes had caused the Band-Aids to loosen and peel from his skin, exposing his ever-growing wound. Eyes widened and voices whispered, but there were no shrieks of horror, so caring and non-judgmental were the workers.

Stanley pressed the Band-Aids back to his face, and now Mr. Elliot handed him the gift and then vanished into the crowd, not to be seen again. It was a long, narrow package wrapped in the shiniest black paper he'd ever seen. With lips quivering and fingers trembling, he managed to tear off the paper revealing a thick box, the words "Cooper's Stationery and Steel" written in Old English Script.

As the workers clapped hands and stomped feet, Stanley carefully opened the box and stared at the gift inside. It was some sort of an antique Bowie knife engraved with the word "Cronus" on the blade.

While Stanley did not understand the significance of inscription, he was overcome by the moment and rose to his feet and ran awkwardly across the floor toward the elevator, gripping his Cronus knife with one hand and snagging his briefcase with the other, leaving the rest of the gifts behind.

It wasn't until he got outside and reached his car that he realized he'd forgotten to give Mr. Elliot the Sampson file.

CHAPTER 12
ASHES

After the emotion of the celebration and the gift of the blade, Stanley couldn't bear the thought of going home and facing his wife and the baby. He also worried that Jeff might have returned from his blue-collar job and that he might walk in on the two of them making love while the baby cried and wallowed in his own filth.

Instead, he drove around aimlessly for a while, tapping his fingers on the steering wheel in time to adult contemporary music, until he finally came to the old strip mall that housed *Lifebridge Drive-Thru Mortuary and Crematorium.* Unlike the last time he'd visited, when he'd had to wait in a line of cars for nearly an hour to witness the body of a stranger, today the drive-thru was closed and the parking lot was empty. Stanley parked in front of the entrance and stepped out of his car, the air quiet and still.

On the door of the mortuary, beneath the name of the business, was a garish painting of Jesus, Moses, and Mohammed holding hands while above them doves fluttered toward a heavenly sky. To the right of the door, a window was damaged by a half-dozen spider web cracks. It was the strangest mortuary he'd ever seen, and Stanley didn't know why he was there, other than the fact that he was fascinated by the viewing he'd seen the other day. And, perhaps, he was also fascinated by the mortician with his faraway gaze and his pallid skin. What kind of a person would choose to be surrounded by death? To prepare bodies that weren't made to last? To drain blood and replace it with formaldehyde? Not him. Certainly not him.

He yanked on the door, but it was locked. He noticed a doorbell, and he reached out and pressed the button but didn't hear a sound. For several moments, he just stood there, and then he pulled the Cronus knife from his pocket and stared at it, his flesh shivering with an unnamed dread. A moment later, he heard footsteps and he stuck the knife in his pocket and took a step back as the door creaked open. A man stood there, but it wasn't the slender gray-haired mortician from the other day. This man was much younger. He had white hair and pinkish skin—an albino. His blue eyes appeared translucent, and while one of them was centered, the other drifted toward the corner of his eye socket. He wore a butcher's apron which seemed to be splattered with blood.

"I'm sorry to bother you without making an appointment," Stanley said. "You see, my father just passed away, and I'd like some information on burials. Would you be able to help me?"

The strange man just stared at him with his one good eye. Then he moved back and nodded for Stanley to enter.

Inside the mortuary, the floor was carpeted white. On the far wall was a television playing an image of a roaring fire. There was a single armchair, also white, in the middle of the room. Otherwise, it was empty. The albino gestured for Stanley to sit down and he did. Then he wiped his hands on his bloody apron several times before walking away, his left leg dragging behind in a slight limp. He opened a door adjacent to the television and disappeared into another room.

Stanley sat there for a long time, staring at the image of the fire. He crossed his legs, uncrossed them, and re-crossed them again. He glanced at his watch but immediately forgot the time, so he checked again. He tapped his foot and closed his eyes. Maybe twenty minutes had passed before he decided this was a bad idea and that he would leave. But he'd just gotten to his feet when the back door opened and a figure appeared into the glow of yellow light. It was the mortician he'd seen the other day, still wearing the same black suit and gray tie and white gloves.

"Aha," he said, sticking out his gloved hand. "I'm Dr. Wagner. A pleasure."

Stanley shook his hand and nodded his head. "I'm Stanley Maddox. I saw you the other day. At the viewing for Mr. Vielle."

Wagner's eyes widened. "Ah, yes. A brown Buick Seville. A quote from Genesis. Regarding dust."

"That's an amazing memory, Doctor. I'm impressed."

Dr. Wagner smiled kindly. "Don't be amazed, sir. It's a sufferance. Have you heard of hyperthymesia."

"Hyper—?"

"Hyperthymesia. A condition where one remembers everything from the past. It can be a burden when I want to forget. But you don't have this problem, do you, Mr. Maddox?"

Stanley shook his head. "No, sir. Quite the opposite, really. I don't remember the past, hardly. And not only that. People don't remember me."

"Then we are a perfect pair. Yes, Mr. Maddox, I remember you quite well. As if you were family." Wagner adjusted the knot on his tie before blinking seven or eight times rapidly. "Now then. I understand you want to discuss burial plans for your father?"

"Yes, sir. That is—"

"Wonderful. I'm the man to talk to. And I apologize that you had to deal with my assistant, Kurt. He's an odd duck to be certain, but I have a certain responsibility for him. I consider him my son."

"I see…"

"But the loss of your own father. It must have been devastating."

Stanley nodded his head and cleared his throat and tried

describing the night in question, but Dr. Wagner wasn't interested in hearing the details.

"I know all about it," he said. "Your father died from complications of tuberculosis."

"Yes, sir. But how did you know?"

"The dead are my business, Stanley. But before we discuss his arrangements, would you mind if I showed you my treasures?"

"Your treasures?"

"Certainly. Follow me, sir. It is so rare to have visitors here with a pulse." He laughed at his own joke.

The walls of the hallway were painted bright blue and red, the primary colors one would expect in an elementary school, not a mortuary. Every so often, Wagner would spot a crumpled piece of paper or a chunk of dirt, and he would bend down, pick it up, and stuff it in his pocket.

It seemed that the hallway extended forever, but eventually they came to a door on the right side with the words "Do Not Enter" written in a child's scrawl. Wagner unlocked the door with an oversized key, and Stanley followed him inside.

"Our embalming room," Wagner explained.

And so it was. There were mortuary trays for transporting corpses, an autoclave for sterilization, and a sink for draining blood. In the middle of the room was an embalming machine, and on the far wall was a mortuary refrigerator containing twelve drawers, temporary housing for the dead.

Without warning, Wagner pulled open one of the drawers. Inside was a young woman—she couldn't have been older than twenty—her face white, her throat slit in a nasty grin.

"Gabrielle Robins," he said. "So lovely. So dead. Another victim of the Midnight Monster. Soul fluttering in the gloom."

Another drawer and another corpse. This one a man with a thick red beard. His jaw was slack, and his tongue was blue and bloated. The same slit on his throat.

"Ed Kramer. A father of three. An electrician by trade. It breaks your heart, doesn't it?"

Wagner showed Stanley another three corpses, and it was a powerful feeling, seeing the human body in all of its putrefaction beauty, knowing that our time to love and hate was so short, and that our time beneath the dirt was eternal.

"But enough of that," Wagner said. "Let me show you my beautiful rewards, purchased on a debit card funded by our Midnight Monster. While many long for peace on earth, morticians long for disease and violence. The capitalism of rotting flesh."

Wagner strode to a corner desk and grabbed an old crowbar wrapped in black electrical tape. As if it was the most normal thing in the world, he got down on his knees and placed the metal tip in between a pair of floorboards. Once the fissured end was safely beneath the board, he rose to his feet and stepped on the bar which lifted the floorboard from the foundation with a loud crack. Without comment, he repeated this process with another five boards until there was a gaping hole in the floor. "I have to keep my treasures hidden," he said. "Otherwise the corpses might snag them." He got down on his stomach and reached into the hole and, accompanied by a few grunts and groans, removed a large rusted metal box.

Now Wagner folded his legs beneath him and placed the box on the floor in front of him. Before opening it, he gazed up at Stanley and said, "I hope you won't think me materialistic. In the past year I have donated fifteen percent of my earnings to various charitable causes, including The Institute of Noetic Sciences. But this year, with the emergence of the Midnight Monster, as well as a nasty strain of influenza, our profits have soared to unimagined heights. I offered to increase Kurt's salary, but he refused, preferring to continue his ascetic lifestyle residing in his shack by the landfill. So I bought some things. Some treasures as I said. Forgive me for my excitement of your arrival, but things tend to be quiet around here. Deathly quiet. I'm sure you'll find the objects… interesting."

Wagner opened the box but shielded Stanley from peeking.

For an instant, Stanley worried that he might have hidden baby corpses beneath the floorboards, so he was relieved when Wagner pulled out some type of a drawing, protected by a plastic sleeve. He handed the artwork to Stanley who studied it, his eyes narrowing to slits. It was an amateurish drawing of a clown with blue triangles painted around his eyes and a red crescent around his mouth. He wore a blue pointed hat and a clown's ruff. Stanley didn't know what he was looking at and could only shake his head.

"You don't recognize the artwork?"

"No. I'm sorry."

"John Wayne Gacy," Wagner said. "An evil soul. He tortured and killed thirty some young men. And, once in prison, he produced some truly bizarre artwork. Elvis, the Seven Dwarfs, Charles Manson, to name a few of his favorite subjects. I bought this clown drawing for eight thousand dollars from the Arts Factory Gallery in Las Vegas. A real steal if you ask me."

"Yes," Stanley said. "It's remarkable."

Stanley handed him back the artwork and now Wagner revealed another piece of paper, this one with a single signature on a piece of stationery. A beautiful calligraphy signature. Albert Fish.

"Who is Albert Fish?"

"Another distasteful man. Known as The Werewolf of Wysteria. Cannibalism, coprophilia, urophilia. You get the idea. He was only caught when he sent the authorities a letter detailing how he choked her to death, then cut her in small pieces so he could eat her virginal meat…"

"It's terrifying," Stanley said.

"Indeed it is. And you'll forgive me for my morbid sensibilities. Part of the job, I suppose."

From there, Dr. Wagner shared more and more memorabilia. A Christmas card from Ted Bundy. A lock of hair from Charles Manson. A windbreaker owned by Richard Ramirez, the Night Stalker. A brick fragment from Ed Gein's hardware store. And so on.

"I thank you for showing me these treasures," Stanley said, "but I'd like to know about my father. That is—"

"Of course! Of course! I apologize for my insensitivities. You know, the film Psycho was based on that madman Ed Gein. Perhaps I will purchase a madman's brain one day. Perhaps yours!"

"Mine?"

A quick pivot. "But you want to know about your father. You want to know if he's in these very coolers, shivering in the cold."

Stanley nodded his head. "Yes. I haven't been very proactive in making funeral arrangements. Everything happened so quickly."

Wagner smiled and squeezed Stanley's shoulder. "Yes. That's how death is. Sneaks up on you in the autumnal woods. But you should breathe easy. No funeral necessary. Only flesh for the fire."

"Excuse me?"

"Cremation, my boy. Perhaps you knew this, but your father did not believe in the bodily resurrection. Perhaps his faith was shaken when you gave into your sinful nature? Would you concede that's a possibility? But now none of that matters. I will bring you to the crematorium. There you will watch the fire. There you will smell the bones. And there you will choose the urn and collect the blackened flesh."

After Wagner returned the box beneath ground and hammered back in the floorboards, they left the embalming room and continued down the long, narrow hallway. As they walked, Stanley peeked into several of the rooms. In one room he saw empty nameplates for funeral wreaths, in another a row of pine coffins, and finally a crematorium chapel where an impossibly old woman dressed in black kneeled in front of a statue of the Redeemer, sobs gagging her breath.

Finally, to the crematorium itself, an empty room save for the terrifying furnaces. One of them was glowing red, and that's where his father burned.

Wagner pointed at the furnace and grinned slyly. "Eighteen

hundred degrees," he said. "Burns the skin and hair, chars the muscles, vaporizes the soft tissues, and calcifies the bones so that they crumble. Ashes to ashes, as you said."

Wagner located a pair of chairs from the corner, and the two of them sat down and stared at the glowing window; it was as if they were sitting around a campfire.

Sensing Stanley's trepidation, Wagner said, "We should not fear cremation, dear Stanley. I find it a much holier process than embalming. Truth be told, I still find it rather ghastly to stare into the empty eyes of a corpse, veins drained of blood, soul already fluttered away. But this fire is rather beautiful, isn't it?"

"Yes," Stanley said. "It is."

And so they watched in silence for an hour and then another and it was a spiritual time, and it had been a long time since Stanley had felt a kinship like this. When the cremation was done, the flames receded and Wagner opened the doors and removed the trays of bone fragments. Whistling while he worked, he placed the fragments into the cremulator (a blender for bones), and within a few minutes they had been pulverized into a sand-like consistency. The bone remains were combined with the rest of the ashes and placed in a decorative urn, classic pewter. Wagner handed the urn to Stanley and nodded. "Your father. Finally home."

Stanley thanked Wagner for the ashes. Then, feeling somewhat awkward, he built up the courage to ask the mortician if it would be possible to meet up under other circumstances. "Perhaps for a cup of tea."

Wagner smiled kindly and said, "Yes. I would like that very much. You know where to find me."

Urn in hand, Stanley turned to leave, but before he'd reached the crematorium doors, Wagner called his name. Stanley stopped and turned around.

"My dear Stanley. I have a request of you. But I fear it may sound strange."

Stanley took a step forward and nodded. "No need to censor

yourself. Anything you ask, Doctor. You saved my father's soul, even if it was too late for my mother. It's the least I can do."

"Yes, then. Well. Would it be possible for me to have a lock of your hair?"

Stanley was understandably surprised by the request. "Excuse me? A lock of my hair?"

"Indeed. For my collection."

"But why?"

"I have a feeling about you, Stanley. Just a lock of your hair. I imagine it will be priceless someday."

CHAPTER 13
THE LAST SUPPER

Having watched his father burned in the retorts and having given the mortician a chunk of his hair, Stanley was famished. Chili's, The Village Inn, or Denny's were all scrumptious choices, but he decided on the new Red Robin Restaurant, the building glittering red and yellow, hatchbacks and SUVs and minivans squeezed into the recently painted parking lot. For several minutes he drove around the lot, ignoring those spots in front of TCBY (too far a walk), until he found a prime one in front of Qdoba's, which was catty-corner to the restaurant.

Before he stepped out of the car, he spent a few minutes gazing at the urn and then at his new Bowie knife, the sharpened metal glinting in the sunshine. He placed the knife in the glove compartment box, away from the eager eyes of thieves and harlots.

He walked across the pavement, thoughts turning to the Midnight Monster etc. etc. When he stepped inside the restaurant, air conditioner blasting, he was happy to see that it was very busy, hopping even. He wasn't at all annoyed when the teen with the Red Robin hat and the vacant stare handed him a buzzer and told him it would be fifteen or twenty minutes but he could certainly sit at the bar and order a beer or a diet soda. He declined, sitting, instead, on a red pleather chair, listening to Taylor Swift on the speakers and watching the waitresses glide across the floor with their trays of sodas and burgers and fries.

He'd drank a lot of soda at the baby shower, and now his bladder was twitching and he needed to use the bathroom. Gripping the buzzer in his left hand, he wandered through the restaurant, inhaling the sweet scent of grilled meat and deep-fried potatoes. As he walked, he paused at each table and listened to a moment of their conversation. He'd become quite expert, through the years, at listening as though he didn't listen, at being a part of their lives without their knowledge.

At one table sat a man with curly red hair and a woman with the same. Husband and wife, and maybe the years living together had caused them to look alike. "The way I figure it," the man said, "there's no better time to install those hardwood floors. Heck, Home Depot is offering white ash planks for seven bucks a square foot. Figure it'll go great with the new countertops."

"But what about the fireplace, Richard? Don't you think white ash will clash with the chestnut oak?"

And then at the next table, a whole family of towheads: "I'd like to keep the carpet in the den, though. Give us a place to play games and such."

And at the next one: "Do you want the oil-based urethane? It'll take a long time to dry, but it'll have more luster."

The same conversation at every table. Hardwood floors. Types of woods and stains. Matching countertops. That was the way of Forest Grove. That was the way of the world.

He finally located the bathroom and relieved himself a couple of urinals down from a gentleman in a tweed coat. While he went, Stanley stared at the wall in front of him and tapped his foot. When he was finished, he zipped up his pants and flushed. But when he glanced over, he saw that Mr. Tweed was staring at him, his jaw slack with disgust. Stanley stood there for a moment, staring back at the man. It seemed that forever passed before he raised his hand and pointed at Stanley. "Your face," he said. "There's something the matter with your face."

Stanley blinked a few times and then his hand instinctively reached toward his face. The Band-Aids, adhered to conceal his wound, had somehow fallen off. Panicked, he turned and faced the mirror and then took a few steps forward.

His eyes widened and he shook his head. The lesion had spread to nearly half his face. A cloudy and foul-smelling fluid was leaking from the wound, and the skin was hot to the touch. He needed to see a doctor, of course. Maybe he had AIDS or some sort of flesh-eating bacteria. He'd rush to the doctor just as soon as he finished his meal...

The man at the urinal had left the restroom, and Stanley grabbed a handful of paper towel and did his best to clean the wound with soap and water. Then he placed more dry paper towel against the side of his face so people wouldn't stare when they saw the grotesqueness. Instead they would think he had perhaps cut his face shaving or was trying to soothe a sunburn. He'd seen worse, certainly. Like the greeter at the Wal-Mart with the enormous goiter on his neck or the black woman at the post office, her face paled by vitiligo. No, a man pressing paper towel to his face wasn't particularly disturbing.

He'd placed the buzzer in his back pocket and now it vibrated. His table was ready. He pushed open the bathroom door with his free hand and moved quickly through the restaurant. There were new conversations at the tables—all about lawns and landscaping.

"That's the mistake too many of our neighbors are making. Cutting the grass too short. You don't want to go shorter than three inches if you ask me. Especially if it's that warm weather buffalo grass..."

"What we need to do is get some mulch—maybe gorilla hair. Be a nice contrast with the pea gravel. If you want, we can even use blue fescue as a clear separation line…"

"I'm going to trim back the juniper bush. It's started to creep onto the driveway and is covering up the granite gravel…"

"How about planting some sort of a shade tree? Maples grow fast, or maybe a tulip poplar…"

And now Stanley thought of his own lawn and his own juniper and he decided that he would need to spend a long weekend getting the property back in shape. Just as soon as he took care of the ever-expanding wound on his face…

He returned to the front counter and handed the vacant-eyed hostess his buzzer. She showed no affect—she didn't seem to notice the oversized paper towel pressed against his face—so Stanley smiled and said, "It vibrated. I think my table is ready."

"Yes," she said. "Follow me."

He chased after her in a zigzag around the tables, and now they were discussing outdoor cooking. The hostess walked to the back of the restaurant and pushed open a door which led to a room Stanley didn't know existed, sterile and filled with overflow seating and fluorescent lighting.

Even though all of the tables were empty, the hostess chose to sit Stanley in the corner, crowded against the wall. She dropped the oversized plastic menu on his table and didn't bother to pick it up when it slid to the ground.

"Meg will be your waitress," she said. And then she left.

He sat there for a moment and then reached down and picked up the fallen menu. With one hand still pressing the paper towel to his wound, Stanley flipped through the menu, his mouth literally watering at the meal descriptions:

Whiskey River® BBQ: A smoky, tangy tribute to the Wild West. Bourbon-infused Whiskey River® BBQ sauce, crispy onion straws, Cheddar, lettuce, tomatoes and mayo.

A.1.® Peppercorn: Hardwood-smoked bacon, melted Pepper-Jack, A.1.® Peppercorn Spread, tomatoes and crispy onion straws on an onion bun, making this burger worthy of five stars.

Chili Chili™ Cheeseburger: You might need an extra napkin. Served open-face with a generous helping of Red's Chili Chili™, Cheddar cheese, chipotle aioli and diced red onions.

And so on, and so on.

He decided on the *Whiskey River® BBQ,* and imagined himself biting into the burger, the red sauce dripping down his chin. He couldn't recall ever being so famished, so he was agitated when there was no sign of Meg, the waitress. Not only was he hungry but he was thirsty and the hostess hadn't bothered even leaving him with water.

How much time passed? Fifteen minutes? Twenty? Thirty? More? It was terrible service, no question about it. Finally, he got out of his seat and pushed open the door to the main dining area. He was infuriated to see that there were several waitresses standing just outside of the kitchen, chatting and laughing, seemingly care-free. He assumed one of them was Meg, probably the one with the upturned nose and yellow hair tied in a sloppy ponytail. He could understand the slow service if they'd been slammed, balancing plates on heads, but that obviously wasn't the case.

He approached the group of waitresses, jaw and fists clenched. They didn't look up when he stood in front of them, didn't look up when he said, "Excuse me. Is one of you Meg? This is, without doubt, the most disgraceful service I can recall ever receiving." No response, not even a bit of eye contact. One thing was clear: the staff at Red Robin didn't care one bit about Stanley Maddox and his feelings and needs.

Well, if that was the case, he would leave and never return. He'd take his business elsewhere, most likely to Chili's. With rage causing his skin to redden, he reached out and slapped the soda from the blonde's hand, the ice and liquid spreading across the floor.

A few gasps, some cackling laughter, and now Stanley kicked the restaurant door with his heal causing the glass to shatter. He staggered out of the restaurant, feeling light-headed and nauseated. For a moment, he considered grabbing the knife out of the car and returning to the restaurant to make a real scene. But when he stepped in the car and opened the glove compartment box, he was disappointed to find that his knife was gone, and so were the ashes.

CHAPTER 14
THE PERSECUTION

And so he drove. Looking at his face in the rearview mirror, he was convinced that he was indeed suffering from some type of flesh-eating disease. He'd been a fool to wait this long, and pretty soon his entire face would be a mess of flesh and pus. So he decided that he'd drive to the nearest hospital and have them take a look, prescribe a powerful antibiotic. His stomach growled, but he could survive another hour or two without eating. After all, hadn't Anastasia of Sirmium survived for two months after being sentenced to death by starvation?

As he drove down the avenue, past one strip mall after another, he thought about his wife and how he could make things right again—most likely by buying some flowers (Lavender Fields Mixed Flower Bouquet—VASE INCLUDED!) and a Hallmark Card (It's the time of year / that the world opens / to all kinds of beauty/ the way you open my world / to all kinds of love). That was the magic of life—it was never too late to make things right again.

That's what he told himself over and over and over again until he was parked outside of St. Anthony's Hospital, a bland monstrosity of architecture, all gray concrete and submarine windows. As he walked toward the entrance, he could sense all of the bystanders' eyes gazing at him, mouths hanging open in horror. He hurried through the automatic doors and walked through the waiting area filled with stiff chairs and flickering television sets. Even though he was inside a hospital, he was still shocked at the number of wounded and diseased. He saw a man lying on the floor, pale and shivering, covered by an Oriental rug; an old woman, clumps of hair missing from her scalp, left leg broken grotesquely; twin girls, both of them sobbing uncontrollably, one of them bleeding from her stomach; an obese man wearing a surgical mask, wheezing and coughing. Meanwhile, in the midst of all the pain and suffering, a pair of gray-headed doctors stood in a doorway, joking and laughing.

Hesitantly, Stanley approached the front desk where an older woman with a ragged bouffant and a red and wrinkled bosom rested her head on her folded arms. Her eyes were closed and her shoulders were rising slowly. Apprehensive about waking her, Stanley stood at the desk for several moments, clearing his throat, but not saying a word. Finally, a troll of a woman told Stanley to shove over and proceeded to slam her fist on the table. The nurse jerked awake, the left side of her face red and creased. The troll cleared her throat and said, "This man wants to be seen." Then she looked up at Stanley and said, "Looks like flesh-eating disease to me."

"Yes," the registering nurse said, patting her bleached hair. "If you'd just like to sign some paperwork."

Stanley turned and thanked the troll, but she only shrugged her shoulders and gazed at him with contempt.

Stanley quickly filled out the paperwork, although for some reason he couldn't remember his date of birth or his phone number, and now his face was burning and he could feel the discharge trickling down his chin. The sleepy nurse glanced over the paperwork and told him to take a seat, and he did, right next to the sobbing twins.

But it was no different than the Red Robin in that he waited and waited, and nobody paid him any mind. He covered his ears to muffle the sobs of the twins, but he could still see the various grotesqueries, and they could see his.

Actually, it didn't seem that *any* of the patients were being seen. The moaning and screaming and sobbing continued, but the registering nurse went back to sleep and the doctors went back to laughing. More patients arrived—one clutching his chest and convulsing, another with a nail driven through his palm (oh, Father, why have you forsaken me?), and another foaming at the mouth. Compared to the rest of these incurables, perhaps his disappearing face wasn't so bad…

In fact, after witnessing all this suffering, Stanley was ready to return to the front desk, wake the nurse, and let her know that he was leaving, that he was voluntarily giving up his place in line. He could get more adhesive pads. That would do the trick for the time being. But at that very moment, a tall and severe-looking woman (how much, minus the green complexion, she resembled the Wicked Witch of the West) approached him, pushing a wheelchair.

In a voice as deep as a man's, she said, "Stanley Maddox?"

He nodded his head. "Yes. That's me."

In her hand, she held an identification tag. But instead of placing it around his wrist, she bent down, removed his shoe and sock, and tied it around his toe. Just like a corpse. Then she straightened up and commanded him to get into the wheelchair.

Stanley wasn't sure if she was joking, and he smiled kindly. "I thank you, ma'am, but the wheelchair is completely unnecessary. You see, there is nothing wrong with my legs. There is nothing wrong with my equilibrium. It's just my face that's causing me problems…"

But the woman was insistent. "Hospital policy," she said. "You'll need to get in the wheelchair, sir. If you need assistance, that can be arranged."

"Please," Stanley said, still smiling, still lighthearted. "I'm perfectly capable of walking. I'm not an invalid."

But when Stanley rose to his feet, the wicked witch used her forehand to shove him back down. Then she moved in close to where Stanley could smell the bologna on her breath. "It would be better," she rasped, "if you follow instructions."

Just then, a pair of male orderlies appeared, both of them with 1950s flattops and sleeves rolled above bulging biceps.

"Fine," Stanley said. "If it will make you happy…"

The two burly men moved to either side of him and then each grabbed an arm. It was in this manner that they lifted him from his seat and placed him not-so-gently into the wheelchair. There was a smattering of applause from the waiting wounded. They were thrilled, perhaps, that one of them had been rescued from the purgatory of the waiting room.

The wheelchair was old-fashioned and had a leather belt that was fastened across Stanley's lap. Once it was secure and there was no way for him to escape, the two orderlies vanished, and then the wicked witch got behind the old wheelchair and proceeded to push Stanley through the carpeted waiting area and toward the black-and-white checkered floor of the emergency room.

But it seemed to Stanley that this wasn't a typical hospital. The examination rooms were all empty, and now that they were far enough away from the waiting area, the hospital became strangely silent with only the sound of the wheelchair click-clacking down the linoleum floor.

Eventually, they came to a long hallway that seemed to lead away from the emergency room and into another building entirely. Here the floors and walls were all white, and there were dozens of portraits of old white doctors with folded arms and stern expressions.

The nurse (witch) didn't speak at all, and Stanley didn't think it would be appropriate to ask any questions. He was hungrier than ever and that only added to his annoyance. He longed desperately for the *Whiskey River® BBQ Burger.* If only he had been politer with the wait staff instead of losing his temper and wanting to slice their throats…

Eventually, they came to an empty examination room and the nurse pushed him inside. There was a small desk, a couple of chairs, and an exam table. But what made the room strange was that all the walls were mirrored, making the space seem infinite.

The nurse now grabbed Stanley's wrist and felt for his pulse, all the while staring at her oversized watch. But instead of the typical fifteen or thirty seconds, she stared at the watch for a good three or four minutes at least.

"142 beats per minute," she finally said. "Dangerously high. Dr. Fuller will be here to see you shortly."

And then she left, closing the heavy door behind her.

Stanley sat in the wheelchair, and he didn't think he'd ever been so frightened. In every direction he looked, he saw his face from different angles, and it was horrid, the stuff of nightmares. He tried unbuckling the wheelchair belt, but he was unsuccessful. And now he wondered if the walls were two-way mirrors and if the doctors from the portraits stood behind them watching him like a goldfish.

But he didn't have much time to feed his fears because the door soon opened and a man that looked nothing like the doctors on the walls entered. He wasn't old—he couldn't have been past thirty—and he wasn't white—his skin almost bluish-purple.

He wore an old-fashioned head mirror as well as a stethoscope. He carried a clipboard, empty of paper. Upon entering, he leaned against one of the mirrors and stared at the clipboard for several moments, his lips moving as if he were reading a file.

Stanley remained in his wheelchair, skin tingling with dread.

"There seem to be some suspicions about you," the doctor said in an accent that Stanley couldn't place.

"I'm sorry?"

"I've done some research. I spoke to several of your coworkers at Evergreen Lending. They didn't have many kind words for you. Most of them said it wouldn't surprise them one bit if you were hiding something terrible. An addiction to pornography, for example. Or a fondness for wearing women's clothing. How do you respond to such accusations?"

Stanley was taken aback and felt disheartened. Why, just that morning they'd thrown him an enormous party, a baby shower, with cake and presents and balloons. And now this. You couldn't trust people. They'd say one thing to your face and something completely different behind your back.

"They don't know me," Stanley said. "Not really. Nobody knows me."

"What about your wife? She said something very similar. She also said that you tended to be abusive, that you got physical with her on a number of occasions. She said that once you tried strangling her. And another time you yanked her hair from her scalp. She said these things and more."

"They're lies," Stanley said, but his heart wasn't into it. His stomach was aching from hunger and the mirrors were causing him to feel disoriented. He knew, however, that he couldn't let this doctor bully him, so he sighed deeply and said, "What isn't spoken of, what isn't mentioned, is that my wife—the very one who claims that I'm abusive—is herself patently dishonest. Did you know, sir, that she's been carrying on an affair for some time now? His name is Jeff. I have reason to believe that our own child, who Wendy named Ian for some reason, is not my own flesh and blood. You see, Dr. Fuller, or whatever your true name and profession may be, I happen to be sterile. So what conclusion would you draw? Are you willing to trust her word—an adulteress—over mine? Is that the way things work around here?"

Stanley felt good about his words. He'd shown Dr. Fuller the fallacies of his thinking. Still, the doctor only smiled and then removed a syringe from his bag. Before Stanley could say another word, the needle was buried in his neck. His eyes rolled back into his head and his tongue lolled in his mouth. He was gone.

***

It was difficult to know how long he was unconscious, but when he woke up, he was still in his wheelchair and was now surrounded by four white faces. The black doctor, Dr. Fuller, was gone, and he wondered if these were the same doctors whose portraits hung on the hospital walls.

"He's awake," one of them said, his voice gravelly as if from disuse.

"Mr. Maddox?" said another one. "Can you hear me? Do you understand what I'm saying?"

Stanley tried to speak, but no words would come out. His mouth smacked open and closed like some ventriloquist dummy.

A distressing thought entered his skull. Perhaps, while he was unconscious, he'd been operated on, lobotomized even. He'd read about a man named Dr. Walter Freeman who traveled across the country in his lobotomobile, carrying a black doctor's bag containing a hammer and an ice pick. On those patients who suffered from depression or psychosis he would hammer the ice pick into the eye socket and then twist, often leaving his patients in a vegetative state. Was that what had happened to him?

"As our colleague mentioned, we have some concerns. Very serious concerns, indeed. As of yet, we have not called the proper authorities but unless we can get some type of explanation, we will have no choice."

"Explanation?" Stanley tried saying, but instead emitted only a strange shriek.

"Indeed." And now the doctor, his red face contrasting with his grandfatherly white hair, nodded to the man to his left, a man who could very well have been his twin. He was carrying a paper bag with the word "evidence" written in big black letters. He reached into the bag and pulled out a knife—the very one that Stanley's coworkers had presented him only hours ago.

"Is this your knife, Mr. Maddox?"

But since Stanley couldn't speak, since he couldn't move even his head, he couldn't respond.

"And inscribed on the blade, the word Cronus. I… we find that very interesting."

"Very interesting indeed," said a fifth doctor who Stanley hadn't known was there due to the confusing nature of the mirrors. This doctor wore a pair of Pince-nez glasses on the tip of his nose. "Cronus. From Greek mythology. He castrated his father. He ate his children."

"Not me," Stanley wanted to say. "I didn't castrate my father. I would never eat my child. Never, ever, never."

"Of course, this evidence alone would never stand up in court. But what about this?"

And now the red-faced twin removed another object from the evidence bag and it was the urn that held his father's ashes. The doctor unsealed the urn and placed it directly in front of Stanley. Then, his voice grave, he said, "Ashes."

A different doctor, or maybe it was the same one, said, "So we now have now recovered the murder weapon and the body. All that is left is to determine a motive…"

And now they were all frothing at the mouth, and Stanley worried that they would carry out his punishment right then and there, but then a phone started ringing, and the doctors stared at each other in panic and began murmuring unintelligibly. Finally, after ten or more rings, one of them walked across the room and picked up the receiver. He listened for a few moments, nodding his head, before bringing the phone to Stanley.

"It's for you," the doctor said. "A man you know."

Bewildered, Stanley reached out his hand and the elderly doctor handed him the receiver. His wound had started itching, and he resisted the urge to scratch at it. He placed the receiver to his ear, listened to the soft breathing on the other line. He was able to grunt something that resembled "hello."

The voice on the other end was muffled, as if a piece of

cloth were placed against the receiver. "Is this Mr. Maddox? Mr. Stanley Maddox?"

Another grunt in the affirmative.

"Do you live at 1320 Willow Way?"

Grunt.

"My name is Bryan Cooper. I live across the green space from you. You've seen me from time to time, pressing my face against the window. Screaming in agony."

And now Stanley remembered, and he felt a chill run up and down his spine.

"I think you should come to my house," the man said. "I have something to show you. I think it'll be of interest to you. Come as soon as you can. I'll be waiting for you."

Then he hung up the phone. Stanley remained for a long moment, his ear still pressed to the receiver. Then he turned and handed the receiver to the doctor who took it without comment.

"A family emergency," Stanley said, his voice suddenly clear. "I should be getting home."

"Yes," one of the old doctors said. "We can't hold you against your will. But we will be keeping an eye on you. Certainly we will. We suggest you don't leave town. We suggest you refrain from dying your hair in the bathroom of a Texaco station."

"If you could just untie me from the wheelchair."

"Of course. But perhaps first we should take care of that wound on your face."

CHAPTER 15
THE DOPPELGANGER

They didn't do a good job caring for his wound, and Stanley suspected that they were not doctors after all. Instead of using an antibiotic, they used toothpaste. And unable to find an adhesive pad that was large enough to cover the enormous lesion, they used several pads of various odd shapes and then wrapped athletic tape around the entirety of his head, once, twice, until the infected area was completely concealed. After more stern warnings not to leave town, they untied him from the wheelchair and allowed him freedom, or some such thing.

Outside, the sun was lowering in the sky and the air was cool and nostalgic. With terror beating in his shirt pocket, Stanley got into his car and drove across town to Bryan Cooper's house.

From the outside, the house looked identical to his: the same beige color, the same cookie-cutter design. Even the potted plants and Welcome mat were the same. He remembered reading about multiverses and how it was possible that reality was split into a set of parallel streams, and he was about to knock on the door, but the door opened before Stanley's knuckles touched the wood.

The man, Bryan Cooper, was a dead ringer for Stanley, from the receding hairline to the oversized shoes. And not only that, he also wore adhesive pads on his face, although they were on the opposite side of his face. Stanley wondered if the neighbor was wearing the pads to mock him, but then decided he was only being paranoid. He thought once again of quantum physics.

"Stanley," the neighbor said, his tongue flicking from his mouth. "I'm so glad you could make it."

Stanley didn't respond. Everything was strange.

"Come in. I'll show you around. You'll see what the problem is. I don't think it can be solved, unfortunately. I'll show you around."

Without saying a word, Stanley followed his neighbor into the house.

Just as he expected, everything was identical to his. The same furniture, the same television set. The same smells. It was the same house, only a different person lived here, a person named Bryan Cooper who had a wound on the left side of his face instead of the right.

But, no, that was wrong. The house was missing some people. There was no Wendy. No Jeff. No crying baby.

As if reading Stanley's mind, Bryan stopped walking and said, "I want to tell you about my wife and son."

"Okay," Stanley said. It was the first time he'd spoken since entering the house.

"But not yet. Do you want a glass of milk? Or would you prefer whiskey?"

"Milk would be fine," Stanley said.

"That's good. I was like you once."

They went into the kitchen. Stanley sat down, and it was hard to believe this wasn't his table. Bryan opened the cabinet and grabbed a shot glass and a large cup. But he surprised

JON BASSOFF

Stanley by pouring milk in the shot glass and whiskey in the cup. He handed Stanley the milk and sat down, not across from him, but right next to him.

For some time, Bryan didn't speak, just sat there drinking his whiskey. His eyes turned hard and mean, and over and over again he tapped the table with his knuckle. Finally, he spoke.

"If you're like me, you hate the world."

Stanley drank his milk.

"From the time you're young, you're handed a dream, only it isn't yours. Find the right girl. Settle down. Get a job, something secure with good benefits. Move into a house. Make sure it's got four bedrooms so you can grow into it. Make sure it's got the right furniture and the right countertops. A television with surround sound, a double oven. Paint the house one of four colors. Have a child. Grow old. Retire. Play golf. Die."

Stanley wiped his mouth with his sleeve. He eyed Bryan's whiskey and longed for a taste himself.

"That was never my dream," Stanley whispered.

More whiskey and Bryan smiled, but there was no humor in that smile. "I know it wasn't, Stanley. I know it wasn't."

"I wanted to be a musician."

"Yes. That's a dream."

"I wanted to play the trumpet. I wanted to live in New York City maybe. Or Paris. I wanted to wear a porkpie hat."

"Have another shot of milk, Stanley."

"I wanted to stay out all night. I wanted to smoke menthol cigarettes. I wanted to make love to the prettiest ladies, tear the gowns from their bodies. I wanted to sneak away while they slept."

"But no," Bryan said. "But no."

"But no. I found a girl. She was pretty enough. I got a job. Paid enough. I found a house. Big enough. I got the furniture and the countertops. I got the television and the oven. I painted the house beige. And we had a child."

"And he's not even yours."

"That's what I tell myself."

98

"Dreams can come true, Stanley. Don't you believe me? Dreams can come true."

"No. It's too late."

"Come see the baby. Come see my wife."

Stanley remained seated. "I could never do something so terrible. Never, ever. That's not the kind of person I am. My father taught me better. He took me to church and moralized at the dinner table. My mother modeled her good deeds every day of her life. Bringing food to the homeless. Allowing a distant relative to sleep in our house as long as needed. Wiping the tears from my eyes when I failed. And I failed so many times. Over and over and over again. No, I could never do something so terrible."

"But the Midnight Monster could, don't you think?"

"Yes. The Midnight Monster could."

"Then become him. Become the Midnight Monster."

"How? How?"

"It's easy if you listen. You put your right foot in, you put your right foot out. You put your right foot in and you shake it all about. You do the hokey pokey and you turn yourself around. That's what it's all about."

"Your wife. Your child."

"In the basement. Follow me, Stanley. Dreams come true. If you dream hard enough."

Bryan brought his oversized glass of whiskey with him, pausing every so often to gulp some of the poison down before grimacing and pounding on his chest.

This was the same house as his, the same goddamn house, and Stanley followed him through the living room and toward the basement door. Down the stairs they walked, and the first thing Stanley noticed was that Bryan's basement was finished, floors covered with carpet, walls painted light blue. He couldn't help but feel jealous and agitated—how many years had he been thinking about finishing the basement but never going through with it because of difficulties with electricity and plumbing. Perhaps seeing his neighbor with his basement completely finished (look at the door moldings!) would inspire him to move forward with the endeavor. The second thing Stanley noticed was the multitude of rabbits scurrying across the floor or sitting still, eyes alert, nose twitching.

"Why all the rabbits?" Stanley said.

"I couldn't say. Such helpless creatures, don't you think? But that's not what I wanted to show you."

And now they walked through the basement, and Stanley was forced to step over all the furry creatures. On more than one occasion he saw a rabbit that seemed to be wounded, limping, or bleeding, and he thought of the bloody rabbit that he'd seen in his own house, the one that had eventually become his son.

"It's just up ahead," Bryan said. "Through this door."

Through this door. Into the furnace room. Stanley remembered and he felt scared. Bryan turned on the light. And there was the small casket, the very one that had been in his own basement not a week before.

"Time to dream again, Stanley. Time to take the world into your own hands, as they say. Time to take the bull by the horn."

"The casket. That casket."

"Well, sure. Open it up, Stanley. See what's inside."

Stanley took a step forward and then another one. The furnace creaked and groaned. He was disappearing, that much was certain. The photo in his bedroom. The skin on his face. He was disappearing, and he was terrified to see what was in the casket.

While Bryan stood behind him, drinking the last of the whiskey, Stanley got down on his haunches and placed his hand on the casket. His hands wouldn't stop trembling.

"You can be whoever you want to be."

Stanley held his breath and slowly lifted the lid. But it had only gotten an inch or so from the base, when he suddenly dropped it back into place and scurried rearward, like a lunatic cornered. He'd seen blood, he was sure of it. A casket full of blood.

Stanley rose to his feet. His eyes were wild.

"Easy, friend," Bryan said. "What are you getting so worked up about?"

Stanley shook his head. "What did you do? Did you kill the baby? Is that what you did?"

"No, no. It's all a joke, friend. Just barbecue sauce. Nearly two dozen bottles worth."

"I'm no murderer," Stanley said. "I'm just a mortgage loan processor. I work hard at the office. I work hard to be a good husband and father and son."

"Of course you do. Follow that dream, Stanley. It's not too late."

"I'm going to leave now. I'm going home. I'm going to kiss my wife and hold my son. I'm no murderer."

He pushed open the door of the furnace room while Bryan remained where he was, his lips stretched into a grin, the pads now dangling from his face, wound-free. "I know you're not a murderer, Stanley. Not filicide, nor patricide, or matricide."

"Goodbye, neighbor. Don't contact me again. Otherwise, I'll have to call the authorities."

"No, you're not a murderer. But the Midnight Monster. He could take care of all of your problems, don't you think?"

There seemed to be thousands of rabbits now (you can't kill the world) and Stanley high-stepped over them. He ignored the lunatic thoughts in his head and raced up the steps, stumbling near the end, and still he could hear Bryan, his strange neighbor, calling out, "A new world awaits you, Stanley. So much hope and love and murder."

He barreled through the front door and ran toward his own house where his wife waited, and the baby, and the casket.

CHAPTER 16
THE TRANSFORMATION

When Stanley stepped inside, Jeff was standing in the living room, hands limp at his side, staring straight ahead. His eyes were empty, and if it weren't for the occasional blink or his shoulders slowly rising with each breath, Stanley might have thought him dead on his feet.

"Jeff," Stanley said. "Where is my wife? Where is my child?"

But Jeff didn't respond. He only reversed a few steps until his shoulders were against the wall, and then he slid to a sitting position. Stanley thought of his strange neighbor and the casket full of blood, and he worried that his own child had been slain, a crooked slit across his throat.

Stepping past his adversary, Stanley hurried up the stairs. He called out his wife's name, but there was no answer. He remembered photos he'd seen of dead babies, photos from the Holocaust it must have been, and the tears rolled down his cheeks, the sobs sucked from his mouth. He stumbled down the hallway toward their bedroom and now he prepared to see Wendy hanging from a light fixture and Ian choking on his own blood. But no, but no. As he stepped inside, he saw Wendy lying on the bed, her left breast exposed, the baby hungrily nursing from it.

Stanley stood in the doorway and watched. And then Wendy looked up, a dreamy look in her eyes, and smiled. It was the most beautiful scene he'd ever witnessed, God's love personified.

"I was afraid," Stanley said, "that you'd be dead."

It was a strange thing to say, and Wendy only shook her head.

"I was afraid that Jeff had killed you. You and the child."

"Shh. Shh."

"I was afraid that *I* had killed you and the child."

And now from somewhere his parents' grandfather clock could be heard banging six times, although that clock hadn't been passed down, although that clock had been destroyed in the flood.

He breathed deeply. His wife was alive. His son was alive. He wasn't a killer. Ted Bundy was a killer. John Wayne Gacy was a killer. Ali Asghar Borujerdi. Vasili Komaroff. And, of course, the Midnight Monster. But not Stanley. Stanley was a hard worker. He was a good husband. A good son. A good father.

And now he sat on the edge of the bed and watched his wife and his son, and outside the sun began to set, coloring the room a soft yellow. A few more minutes and the baby, little Ian, sweet little Ian, was satiated, and he closed his eyes and slept, occasionally jerking awake to resume his nursing. Soon Wendy slept too, her mouth tugged upward in a Mona Lisa grin.

Stanley closed his eyes. He thought about the madness of his life, and began to sob. It felt cathartic, so much pain burrowed beneath his skin. "No more madness," he whispered. "No more madness." Then he pulled himself forward and lay next to his wife and his son. He listened to them breathe in unison. He smelled the sweet scent of mother's milk. And for the first time in forever, he felt like he was home.

He slept without dreaming, but a few times he opened his eyes to a sky changed to black, a soft rain blurring the window, violin music playing from somewhere. He reached out and touched his wife's shoulder, and she didn't stir. He leaned over and kissed his son's smooth head, and he couldn't believe the wicked thoughts that had once resided in his own skull...

Hours or perhaps days passed and he finally awakened, feeling like a new man, rested and strong and happy. But now his wife and son were gone, leaving only a faint indentation in the pillow.

Instinctively, his hand moved to his face where he had become accustomed to the wound, worsening by the minute. In his long slumber the bandage had come loose, but instead of the throbbing lesion, his skin now felt smooth and wound-free. Could it have really happened? A healing slumber?

Feeling something like joy, Stanley rose to his feet, his hand still caressing his face. He would have rushed to the bathroom and gazed at his cured skin in the mirror, but he was afraid that a single glance would cause the flesh to, once again, peel from his bone. So instead he paced around the bedroom, a wide grin spread across his face, and the grin remained until something caught his eye, the photograph of his wife and him, the photograph that had caused so much consternation.

Stanley moved forward several steps until he was directly in front of the photograph. With his right hand he reached out and touched his fingers to the glass. As he studied the image, he felt a coldness rise up inside of him.

The image of him had completely vanished.

Now, Wendy stood alone, still wearing her lovely blue dress and white Easter bonnet, still holding a bouquet of daisies. But he was gone.

He was devastated because he knew the symbolic nature of this development. So he did this: he removed the photograph from the wall. Then, mustering up a scrap of rage, Stanley slammed it to the ground, the glass shattering into a thousand shards. The joy, so brief, was gone. Gone forever. He picked up one of the slivers and pressed it to his forearm, drawing blood. He needed to hurt, he needed to bleed.

An impulse. He removed his shoes and socks. Then he gathered up as many of the shards as possible and placed them inside the socks. He pulled them back on, and he screamed in agony. Then his shoes, and he was being punished.

The glass slicing into the soft skin of his arches, Stanley limped toward the door and out of the bedroom. He called for his wife. He called for his child. The house was quiet.

Down the hallway he staggered until he came to the final door, which had long been a storage closet but had now been transformed into Ian's nursery. The walls were painted light blue. There was a dresser and changing table and a cream-colored glider with picture books stacked on top of one another. And then there was the crib where Wendy leaned over, singing an olden lullaby.

Stanley moved forward, his feet bloody for sins not yet committed.

> *Above black eagles wheeling,*
> *All of a sudden swooping,*
> *My little baby stealing,*
> *Sleep, little baby, sleep.*

Closer and closer, and still she sang.

> *Above black birds ascending,*
> *My baby's flesh a-rending,*
> *And all the world attending.*
> *Sleep, little baby, sleep.*

He whispered her name, *Wennnnddddy*, but something wasn't right. The voice wasn't his. *Wennnnddddy.*

Slowly she turned around, and now Stanley saw that she was wearing the same blue dress, the same white bonnet as from the photograph. She looked at Stanley for a long moment and her expression changed from placid to terrified. She raised her arm in the air, her finger pointing accusatorially at Stanley. Then her mouth opened and an awful shriek arose from her throat and echoed against the walls. And as soon as that shriek was finished, she took a deep breath and did it again and again.

Stanley, for his part, covered his ears and gritted his teeth. Then he slowly backed out of the room. Wendy grabbed her child from the crib and held him to her chest, protecting him from the evil that she now perceived.

When Stanley got to the hallway, he could hear voices and the clatter of footsteps. He peered down the stairs and saw a group of men, all wearing black overcoats. He quickly recognized them as the doctors from the hospital. One of them was carrying his father's ashes. One of them was carrying the Cronus knife. When they saw him, they pointed and shouted, and then they started up the stairs. Wendy had emerged from the nursery, cradling her son, and she ordered the doctors to get Stanley, to tie him with rope and wires until the proper authorities arrived.

Having no other options, Stanley raced down the hallway toward their bedroom. He could hear the doctors behind him. His feet were aching from the broken glass, but still he staggered forward. Inside the bedroom, he managed to open the window and then to kick out the screen. As the doctors entered the room, Stanley crawled out the window and stood on the roof. He was fifteen or twenty feet above the ground, but he didn't hesitate, quickly leaping from the structure and crashing to the yard below.

He'd landed on his shoulder and was sure it was dislocated. He rose to his feet and ran while the doctors chased after him, shouting, "Hey! Stop! We only mean to kill you!" And now he glanced back and saw his adversary, Jeff, standing on the roof with a short-barreled rifle resting on his shoulder, aiming it in Stanley's direction. Then he heard the retort of the rifle, and he worried that his head would explode, but it didn't, and so he kept running through the quiet suburban neighborhood, the doctors, elderly all, falling farther and farther behind.

He hobbled across Briarwood Avenue and into a new neighborhood that looked the same as his own. He could still hear the enraged voices of the doctors, could hear the occasional crack of the rifle and, if he listened very carefully, could hear the sobbing of his own son.

He came to a cul-de-sac, the houses all with oversized garages and neatly trimmed lawns and dying rose bushes. Stanley didn't know where he was running to, but he knew what he was running from. He saw that one of the garages was open. Fearing for his sanity more than his life, he ducked inside. Two cars, both European and expensive, were parked in the garage. There was another bellow from the doctors. Another warning shot from Jeff.

Stanley maneuvered through the garage, stepping over gardening tools, a golf bag, and whiskey crates. He reached the far side and pressed the white button with the palm of his hand and the garage door slowly groaned shut. Worried he would be discovered by the owner of the house, Stanley moved to the corner and hid behind a plastic trash bin. The light remained on.

He stayed in that corner for a long time, breathing deeply, trying to make sense of things. He visualized the photograph, him vanished. He pictured his wife's terrified expression and remembered her awful screams. It was all too much. He wished things could be like they used to be. When the world was peaceful and pretty, and orange leaves crunched beneath his feet. That time existed, he was sure…

Another twenty minutes, and he knew he couldn't stay hidden forever. But he was petrified of returning outside where the doctors waited with their clipboards and Jeff waited with his rifle. After mulling things over, he decided there was nothing else for him to do but go inside the house. He would enter quietly, being sure not to startle whoever resided there. Then he would explain his situation. How he was being hunted for an unexplained crime, how his own wife had been brainwashed to view him unfavorably. He would ask to use a telephone and he would call a relative—didn't he have an Uncle Wyatt in Sarasota?—who would hopefully take him on as a boarder until he was able to clear up the misunderstanding with his wife and the doctors.

Stanley rose to his feet and gritted his teeth. He edged his way through the garage, his breath held, his footsteps soft. From the corner of his eyes, he noticed several flies—five or six or seven of them—spastically trying to enter the house, banging against the door over and over and over again. A few of them managed to squeeze through the bottom of the door, and Stanley wondered about corpses inside.

A few more steps forward, and he glanced to his right and saw a reflection in the car window—a man, his hair white, his face albino. Stanley felt a coldness rise up inside of him. It was Kurt Wagner, the mortician's son.

With a gasp, Stanley spun around, but the albino had seemingly vanished into thin air. He had seen him, he was sure of it. Stanley peered around the garage, looking for movement, but all was still. He breathed deeply and then called out, "Kurt? Mr. Wagner? Is that you?"

No answer.

"My nerves," Stanley whispered to himself. "That's all it is. My nerves."

Shaking his head, Stanley continued toward the door, but with every step he took, he thought he heard footsteps echoing behind him…

He opened the door. From upstairs, he could hear the muted sound of opera. He saw more flies, dozens of them, some buzzing through the hallway, some motionless on the floor and ceiling. And then he noticed a rectangular serpentine mirror hanging crookedly from the wall. As he neared the mirror, he again saw the reflection of the albino, his teeth bared in a sinister grin.

Again, he spun around. Again, nobody was behind him.

"Show yourself," Stanley said. "I know you're here with me."

But as he returned his gaze to the mirror, the truth soon became evident. The reflection of Kurt Wagner was his own.

II

KURT WAGNER

Both sides of me were in dead earnest; I was no more myself when I laid aside restraint and plunged in shame, than when I laboured, in the eye of day, at the furtherance of knowledge or the relief of sorrow and suffering.

—Robert Louis Stevenson, *Strange Case of Dr. Jekyll and Mr. Hyde*

CHAPTER 17
GENESIS 3:19

He didn't scream. He didn't faint. He just shook his head in disgust and squeezed his eyes shut. So this is who I am now, he thought. A man with white hair and albino skin. The son of a mortician. Hands stinking of death.

But while it was true that Stanley was shocked and frustrated with the transformation, it was also true that he was somewhat relieved. With his new countenance and his new body—now lean and gaunt, his beer belly gone—he would no longer be imprisoned by circumstances. No longer would the doctors be chasing him. No longer would his boss be hounding him. No longer would his wife be cheating on him. He thought of his child, Ian, and for a quick moment he mourned the loss of fatherhood, his eyes moistening, but then his lips spread into a grin and he imagined he was happy.

He walked through the hallway and into the living room, his feet aching with every step. Now he remembered the shards of glass in his shoes. Despite his metamorphosis, the soles and arches of his feet remained bloody, the result of his martyrdom.

As he neared the stairs, the sound of the opera became

louder. He wanted to warn the residents that he was here, so there wouldn't be an unwanted shooting. He called out in a quiet voice, "Hello? Is anybody here? My name is Stanley Maddox. Hello? Is anybody here? My name is Kurt Wagner."

Up the stairs he climbed, and it seemed that with every step he took, each of his memories as Stanley Maddox became more blurred, and by the time he reached the top of the steps, they were gone completely.

And now, as if by a wizard's spell, he remembered the things that Kurt would remember, felt the things that Kurt would feel, hated the things that Kurt would hate.

"I remember," he said, without prompting, "the first time I saw a dead body. I was seven years old, and Dr. Wagner had taken me to work. She was lying on a mortuary tray. Her name was Suzanne, and she'd been in a car accident, and her body was mangled, her face charred beyond recognition. I shrunk from the sight, hid in the corner of the room. The doctor only laughed. Then he patted my head and said, 'Let me tell you, boy. I once saw a dog, crazy with rabies, tearing at its own belly until its intestines spilled onto the ground. I was equally traumatized. But it was at that moment when I understood. And I hope you understand as well.'

"'Understand what?' I asked him.

"'That poets and artists and musicians deal in propaganda. That there is no heavenly blue sky, no lovely flowers blooming, no autumn breeze blowing—no beauty at all, only a mass grave ready to swallow and digest our flesh, blood, and bones.'"

Kurt came to the second-floor landing and stood there for a moment. Now, for the first time, he was sure he understood what Dr. Wagner had told him. More flies buzzed around his head, and he thought of that poem:

I heard a Fly buzz – when I died –
The Stillness in the Room
Was like the Stillness in the Air –
Between the Heaves of Storm –

The opera played louder and louder—something by Poulenc, he thought—and Kurt continued down the hallway until he reached the final door. It was only open a crack, and he knew this was where he lay, his dreams filled with mortal terror.

He placed his hand on the doorknob and gently pushed open the door.

The room was cold—Kurt noticed the curtains swaying in the breeze—and was only lit by the dull glow of the streetlights outside. A large older man lay on the bed, sleeping. He was on his back with his hands folded on top of his red and white flannel pajamas. Next to his bed was a nightstand, and on the nightstand was a neatly-combed toupee and a glass that soaked his dentures.

Kurt studied the man whose chest rose with every breath. He walked across the room, the hardwood floor creaking beneath his feet. He sat in a chair next to the old man and for a long time he watched him sleep, thinking, again, about Dr. Wagner's words, how the world was only a grave waiting on the dead. And soon another one.

The opera ended with a shriek and Kurt knew it was time. He reached into his shirt pocket and pulled out his mortician scalpel, his own pallid skin reflecting on the blade. He was about to attack, but when he leaned forward, he saw two confused blue eyes staring back at him. Kurt stopped.

The man pushed up in the bed, his back pressing against the window. He tried speaking, but it seemed that his mouth wouldn't work, and so, lower lip trembling, eyes twitching, he continued staring at Kurt. Caught in the act, the mortician's assistant placed the scalpel on his lap, so as not to alarm the old man.

Finally, words. "Who… who are you?"

"There is no need to be frightened," Kurt said, trying to speak calmly, although his voice was louder than he would have liked. "What you should know, what they haven't told you, is that you're sick, very sick. You don't have long to live."

The man shook his head. "That's not true. Despite some issues with my mental competency, I'm not sick. My name is Robert Elliot and I'm the regional manager at Evergreen Lending. I'm not sick. You're a liar."

It was difficult when they didn't want to go quietly into the night. Resisting only made it hurt more.

"But you *are* sick, Mr. Elliot, and you'll only get sicker." Kurt was surprised at how resolute he sounded. He was always surprised how resolute he sounded. "From your first breath, you were infected, and the disease has gotten worse every minute of your life. There is only one antidote, I'm afraid." And now he looked longingly at the scalpel before returning his gaze to the man's olden face. For quick moments, he wondered about the old man's life. Had he loved? Had he lost? When he was young, had he run through a field of golden leaves, laughing, his face bright with hope? Had he lay on the ground and watched the clouds twisting in an illusory blue sky? Had he fallen in love with a young woman with a mischievous smile? Had he cried with joy when she gave birth to their first and then second child? Had he watched his wife, that same beauty from many years ago, slowly wither away from pancreatic cancer, her final breath rattling in her ribcage?

A single tear fell down the man's cheek. A single tear for the millions of small moments, now disappearing into the thick air. Outside, the streetlight flickered off, and the room was dark.

"No," he whispered. "I don't have a disease. And the world is a good place. God made it. I believe that."

"Yes," Kurt said. "He might have."

"And… and that means all of his creations are good. That you're good."

"No…"

"Please, mister. Whoever you are. Let me live. You don't have to do this."

"How about mahogany?" Kurt said.

"What?"

"For your casket."

The old man only shook his head, and now Kurt could smell the putrid odor of urine. He was sure Mr. Elliot had pissed the bed and for some reason that made him enraged. He slammed his fist against the arm of the chair.

"Why do you look at me without recognizing me?" Kurt said, his voice rising.

"I… I… Am I supposed to recognize you?"

"In the papers. Everyday. My name is Kurt Wagner. But you'd know me as the Midnight Monster."

He nodded his head, now resigned. "Yes. That's right. I know who you are. I always knew."

"I kill not because of fate, but because nothing matters."

"But God—"

"Not God. The Devil." Kurt breathed deeply. "No more talk. Now, it's time."

"No. Please. First tell me. How will you do it? I pray that it won't be too painful?"

Such a stupid question. Kurt looked at Mr. Elliot, this worthless bureaucrat, and felt an intense hatred. "Not too painful. I'll press a pillow to your face. And then I'll slice your throat with my scalpel."

Kurt lifted the scalpel and showed it to the man. More tears fell down his cheeks.

"And… will it be terribly messy? You see my son will be coming soon to check up on me, and—"

It was a negotiation. "Your sheets will be soaked in blood. But I will try to keep the floor clean."

The room was now filled with flies, the same ones Emily saw, and Kurt, a monster, pounced on the poor man, pressing the pillow to his face while he grabbed weakly at Kurt's arms.

Thirty seconds, sixty seconds, and the old man was barely resisting. Kurt pulled the pillow away from Mr. Elliot's face, and he gasped for breath. But it wasn't for long as the Midnight Monster dragged the scalpel across his throat in a movement fluid and practiced. Soon his flannel pajamas were covered with blood and then his mattress. His eyes remained open, the promises of salvation dripping from his veins.

The deed done, Kurt rose to his feet and leaned against the wall. He was breathing heavily, so he located a cigarette and, with steady hands, lit it. He breathed deeply, the smoke crippling his lungs. After a few minutes, Kurt bent down and worked on untying his own shoes. He yanked off the glass-filled socks, soaked with Stanley Maddox's blood. Then he limped across the floor and used the bloody sock to write a biblical message on the wall: For dust you are and to dust you will return.

CHAPTER 18
THE INVESTIGATION

They would find Kurt's DNA on the wall, of course, but that didn't matter because he was invisible, a man without a record, a man of no importance to anybody in the world—not even to Dr. Wagner. Still, he washed his feet in the bathtub, and he did his best to clean up his bloody footprints from the floor because he'd promised Mr. Elliot there wouldn't be a big mess for his son to clean up. He returned his shoes to his feet and stuffed the socks in his pocket.

One of these days he would get caught, and he looked forward to that day because then the world would know who he really was—the Midnight Monster. He had heard that women loved men on death row, often sending them letters and offering conjugal visits. But until that time, he would keep killing because there was nothing else to do. His father's business would continue to boom, and the old man would allow him to keep killing without moral judgment.

How many times had he come home, his clothes splattered with blood, as his father watched the news of another death at the hands of the Midnight Monster? And sometimes the old man would ask him where he'd been, and Kurt would tell him he couldn't remember, and the old man would shake his head and say it sure is a shame about this Midnight Monster, but it isn't hurting business, is it? And then he'd wink. An autopsy by the coroner, and then the body would be delivered to Lifebridge Drive-Thru Mortuary and Crematorium for cremation or funeral preparation. Just another six or so funerals, and the old man would be able to afford The Zodiac Killer's final letter to the press: *Me—37, SFFSD—0.*

But how much he wanted to tell the world! I'm a killer, he'd say—the best there's ever been. Better than the Zodiac Killer, better than Ed Gein, better than Ted Bundy. What would the world think of him then? Would they finally notice him as something more than a grotesque albino?

He took a final look at the corpse, putrefaction not so many hours away. Swarms of flies now filled the room, and he gritted his teeth so as not to allow them to fly in his mouth and down his esophagus.

Before leaving the room, he walked over to the phonograph and placed the needle back at the beginning of the record. He stood there for several minutes with his eyes closed, overwhelmed by the emotion of the music.

But when he opened his eyes, he was surprised to see that the room was no longer empty, instead filled with crime scene investigators. Eight, maybe ten of them, but they didn't seem concerned about Kurt's presence. They were taking pictures, writing notes, and generally milling around.

"Well, I'll be damned," said a fat man with a too-short tie and a balding head. "Looks like the Midnight Monster has struck again. 'And the life of the ebony clock went out with that of the last of the gay.'"

"Who you quoting this time?" asked his partner, this one skinny with an enormous bobbing Adam's apple. "Shakespeare or some shit?"

"No, sir. Edgar Allan Poe. 'The Masque of the Red Death.' You read it?"

"Nah. I don't read. Except for sometimes Patterson."

A couple of young female officers gathered evidence in plastic bags, and a black man hummed a song and dusted the room for fingerprints.

A balding man whom Kurt recognized stood over the corpse. He was studying the wound and mumbling to himself. Dr. Keenan. The medical examiner. But he'd only studied the dead man for a minute or less before he made his pronouncement to nobody in particular. "Robert Elliot. Sixty-six years old. Time of death around midnight. My ruling: homicide from a cut throat. Left to right in motion. Cause of death is asphyxia due to aspiration of blood."

Case complete, he pulled a crumpled death certificate from his shirt pocket and scribbled and stamped it and then handed it to the lead detective. He then removed a flask of something from his trouser pocket, took a long swig and then another one. He nodded at a trio of detectives standing by the door, said, "Gentlemen," and left the room.

The investigators stayed there for thirty or forty minutes, and none of them talked to Kurt until one of the photographers said, "You must be here to transport the body."

"Yes. But how did you know?"

"Because you morticians always look nearly as dead as the corpses themselves."

Evidence gathered, theories promulgated, the lead detective (he with a Fu-Manchu mustache and a Mr. Weatherbee hairstyle) slapped Kurt on the back and said, "He's all yours. A little duct tape to keep his head attached, don't you think?" Then he laughed. Kurt watched as the detective and the rest of the investigators left en masse, ready for their next homicide gathering.

And once again Kurt was alone with the corpse. He now realized that he didn't have a stretcher to carry the old man out and that made matters difficult. Still, he had a job to do and couldn't afford to waste any more time, so he got down on his hands and his knees and maneuvered the corpse until its legs and arms were relatively straight. Then he placed his hands and arms beneath the neck and knees and attempted to powerlift the dead body. It was a struggle, but eventually he managed to gain some leverage and get to his feet, the corpse pressed against his chest.

Weaving like a drunkard, he made it down the hallway and to the staircase. Down the stairs he walked, his arms aching, and along the way he saw a man wearing a white seersucker suit and pressing a handkerchief to his face. Kurt knew from the desperate sobs that this was the old man's son, the one that was here to check up on him. "And was he your father?" Kurt asked because he couldn't think of anything else to say.

The man nodded his head and wiped a tear from his eye. "Yes. He used to comfort me when I cried. He used to wash my mouth out with soap when I cursed. That was so long ago. You're never prepared for the end. Now, when I cry, he won't be there to comfort me."

The man sighed deeply and closed his eyes. He rocked back and forth, and Kurt knew he loved Mr. Elliot very much. He touched the man's shoulder. "Would you like to have a few minutes alone?"

"No," the man said. "I made peace years ago. His soul is with the Lord. His body can go with you."

The man was about to walk past, but Kurt cleared his throat. "I know now isn't the best time, but perhaps we could quickly discuss funeral arrangements? We offer many types of memorials, many types of visitations, many types of graveside services. And it's never too soon to decide on a casket, the place that he'll be spending eternity…"

Back in the living room, all of the curtains were closed and the lights were off, contributing to a sense of gloom. Details he hadn't noticed before: paintings of barns and autumnal scenes on the walls; an accordion of magazines spread across the coffee table. An hour before, Mr. Elliot had been alive. Now he was dead. Kurt pushed open the front door and stepped outside into the cool night, the moon hidden behind blackened clouds, the wind rustling the skinny trees.

To the side of the house there was a shed, and next to the shed there was a wheelbarrow. Without a gurney, without his rusted van, this was the only way. He released his grip and allowed the body to topple into the wheelbarrow. The head dangled over the back and the legs over the front, but it was secure enough. He lifted the handles and pushed the wheelbarrow through the quiet neighborhood, past the twisted cul-du-sacs with their tomblike homes, toward Fillmore Avenue and the mortuary.

Along the way, he passed a woman walking with her child, and when she saw the dead body in the wheelbarrow, she quickly covered the boy's eyes because death is best kept out of sight. "But is that Robert Elliot?" the woman asked. "The poor man. Did you murder him or did he die from natural causes?"

"No, no," Kurt mumbled. "Natural causes. I'm quite innocent. Tuberculosis, I believe. The medics tried to save him, but to no avail."

"It's a shame," the woman said. "I used to see him watering his lawn from time to time. I'd long since forgotten that he was alive, though."

He kept pushing, and after so many long blocks Kurt was getting fatigued. An oversized SUV drove past, stopped, and then backed up. A man wearing khakis and a polo shirt stepped out of the car. He looked at Kurt and the dead man in the wheelbarrow. He shook his head and pulled back his thinning hair with his hand. "A burden in life and a burden in death," he said before returning to his car and driving away.

A handful of other bystanders commented philosophically about life and death, but finally, as the wind blew harder and Robert Elliot's body got colder, Kurt reached Fillmore Avenue, filled with the familiar chain stores and strip malls and car dealerships. Soon he would be at Lifebridge where Dr. Wagner, his father, would be waiting in the crematorium, a cold glass of lemonade in his hand, watching the bodies burn.

The cars raced down the avenue, headlights cutting through the night. Kurt's shoulders, back, and arms were all aching. He decided that there would be no harm in stopping for a few minutes, parking the wheelbarrow in order to rest his weary muscles. He sat down on the pavement, and there wasn't anything illegal about a young man sitting next to a corpse in a wheelbarrow.

But he hadn't been resting for long when he spotted a group of men, all with white hair, all wearing white doctor jackets, moving en masse toward where he was sitting. And in the middle of the group, a big, burly man wielding a rifle. Instinctively, he hid behind the wheelbarrow, behind the dead man. When they saw him hiding, they shouted something unintelligible. Kurt considered rising to his feet and racing away, but he didn't want to draw suspicion, so he remained sitting. He had always been terrified of mobs, and pretty soon they stood in front and behind him, blocking any path of escape.

"Excuse me, sir," one of the grandfatherly men said. A stethoscope dangled from his neck. "I'm sorry to disturb you. You see, we're looking for a man. His name is Stanley Maddox. We believe him capable of doing terrible things. Abuse. Assault. Murder, even. He's balding, heavy set. A grotesque wound on his face. We know he's around here somewhere, although it's possible that he's sneaked into a house and taken a family hostage. We've been searching for him for some time. Have you seen him?"

Kurt shook his head quickly. "No. I haven't seen him."

And now another one of the doctors said, "But isn't that his boss? Isn't that Mr. Elliot?"

"It's possible," Kurt said. And now he rose to his feet and began pushing on the wheelbarrow.

"But why are you in such a rush?" one of them asked. "Where do you need to go?"

"My father is expecting me. At the mortuary. People are always dying. More than they're born, it seems. We need to prepare this corpse, find a suitable casket. I wish I could help you…"

The big man in the middle raised his rifle and pointed it directly at Kurt, causing him to stumble backwards. But then the man grinned and lowered the weapon and all the doctors laughed.

"Well, then," another one of the doctors said. "By all means get back to the mortuary. But please keep your eyes out for this Stanley. We believe he may have killed his own father, perhaps with this very knife." And now he pulled out a knife and showed it to Kurt. It had the word Cronus inscribed on the blade.

"I'll keep my eye out," Kurt said. "Good luck in finding him. I hope he doesn't kill anybody else. Death often leads to damnation, or so I'm told."

"Indeed. But why don't you take the knife with you? You never know in a neighborhood like this when you might need to protect yourself. Suburban angst." The doctor handed him the Cronus knife. Kurt studied it for a moment and then stuck it in his back pocket.

"I thank you, gentlemen. And now goodbye."

So they let him pass, and as he hurried down the avenue, he stole a glance back and saw the old men still searching, peeking in sewers and car windows and storefronts, and he wanted to tell them that Stanley Maddox was gone forever, a feeble man swallowed up by a monster.

CHAPTER 19
THE MAKING OF THE MONSTER

When he finally arrived at the mortuary, the moon and stars were vanished behind clouds blackened with soot, and the rain had started to fall. Kurt was physically exhausted from the long walk, and emotionally exhausted from spending so much time transporting one of his victims. Not wanting to search for the key in his pocket, he took to kicking the glass door, hoping that Dr. Wagner would respond. It took a long time, and now Kurt and the corpse were both soaked from the rain, but the mortician eventually did appear, pressing his face against the blurred glass and then opening the door.

"Oh, Lord," the old man said. "Why are you out in the rain? Why are you transporting a body in this haphazard fashion?"

Kurt staggered inside, his white hair slashed over his eyes. "I found myself inside a stranger's house," he said. "The man was dead. My job is to transport bodies. But I didn't have a stretcher. I didn't have a car…"

"And this man. Did you kill him? Did you kill him like you

have killed so many in the past?"

Kurt shook his head. "I might have, sir. But I am so tired. I need to sleep. Maybe all of this is just a bad dream."

"There's something wrong with you, boy. I will call Dr. Hammond shortly. He understands these things. The way the criminal mind works. But you can't sleep until we prepare the body. The viewing will be tomorrow, certainly. I expect he was a cheerful man with many friends and family members. I expect a long line of cars."

Dr. Wagner left the waiting area in search of a gurney. He returned several minutes later and together they lifted the body—the skin stained black from pooled blood, the throat gaping from the razor—and placed it on the stretcher. The corpse's arms flopped off the side, and Kurt returned them to his chest in a vampire position. Whistling a strange song, Dr. Wagner pushed the gurney through the hallways until they came to the embalming room.

How many bodies had they prepared together over the years? Hundreds, certainly. Thousands, possibly. And how many of those deaths had been caused by the Midnight Monster? Something Kurt knew: it wasn't because of familial duty or love that Dr. Wagner didn't turn him in. It was because the Midnight Monster was good for business.

Most of the time when they prepped bodies they didn't talk, but tonight was different. Kurt felt more melancholy than usual, wishing, perhaps, that he was on the gurney, not Mr. Elliot. As Dr. Wagner prepared the disinfecting solution, Kurt spoke in a somber voice. "I wish I wasn't the way I was, sir. I wish I didn't have to hurt people. I wish I didn't have to kill people. Why am I this way? Why am I the Midnight Monster?"

Dr. Wagner used a scissor to cut off the dead man's pajamas, placing a white pad on top of his genitalia. Mr. Elliot's muscles were contracting beneath his cold skin. The mortician glanced up at Kurt and said, "It is no use wondering. Perhaps it is God's will. Perhaps he has some use for you."

Kurt shook his head. "No," he said. "God has no use for me. But perhaps the Devil."

Dr. Wagner gripped the dead man's hand, and Kurt had the notion that he would rather comfort a corpse than a living man.

"You say the Devil, huh?"

"Yes. The Devil."

The old mortician walked slowly across the room and grabbed a blue spray bottle, filled with disinfecting solution. He sprayed inside the corpse's ears and nose, then he used his gloved hands to pry open his mouth and sprayed his tongue and the back of his mouth.

Without looking up, he said, "But perhaps you want to talk about it?"

Kurt nodded his head. He could feel his eyes welling with tears. "I would. Yes. Perhaps talking might allow me to process…"

Dr. Wagner grunted. He asked Kurt to hand him the needle and thread, and then he got to work on closing the gash on the dead man's throat. As he sewed, his hands were steady. Kurt spoke in a hushed voice.

"I suppose I'll start at the beginning. The first one's name was Carol. I saw her at the indoor mall and took an interest in her. You see, she had bright blonde hair but dark brown eyes, and I found that strange. Maybe her hair was dyed. Or maybe she wore colored contacts. It didn't really matter. I watched her. Her life was mundane, just like everybody's. She worked as a secretary at a law firm. She answered phones and made copies and painted her nails. Every day after work she would go to Hasty Bakery and buy a Danish Pinwheel. She didn't need the calories, but it was tradition. If I had had the guts, I would have told her to cut out the sweets. Lose a little weight and maybe some of the lawyers would have taken an interest. But she never did. She lived in a small brick ranch built in the '50s. Each night she would eat a frozen meal for dinner and read her magazines and watch her TV. She wasn't married, of course. Didn't have a boyfriend. Didn't have any friends at all.

I watched her for several weeks. It was tedious. At some point, I'd had enough..."

As Kurt spoke, Dr. Wagner glanced up every few moments, eyes disinterested. Now he located a jar of mortician's putty and massaged a dab over Mr. Elliot's newly-stitched wound, using cosmetics to blend the putty to the color of his dead skin. Kurt cleared his throat. It didn't really matter if Dr. Wagner was listening. He needed to say these things, to confess these sins.

"It was a night like any other—not rainy or windy or hot and stifling. Just another night. I knew her routine, so at five thirty I entered her house, using the key that she left hidden beneath a watering can. I spent twenty or so minutes wandering down the hallways and through the rooms, hoping to find something of interest. A crumpled letter from an old lover. A vial of pills. A diary. Photographs of her past. Poems of her future. But there was nothing but drawers full of boredom and I wondered why she bothered, why anybody bothered. I was staring at her goldfish when I heard the front door squeaking open, and so I quickly hid under her bed. She entered the house, her high heels muffled by the carpet, and I could hear her talking to herself: 'Oh, dear, it's awfully chilly in here. I wonder if I left a window open?' And: 'I still need to call the plumber about that leaky faucet.' And so on. For the next two or three hours I listened to her prattling, milling, eating, and finally watching a program on television, the laugh track echoing against the lonely walls."

The old man smiled. He took a step back and stared at the corpse, admiring his work. Then he moved forward again and worked on breaking the rigor mortis by massaging the body and loosening joints.

Kurt continued: "I waited until she'd taken her shower and put on her nightgown. Waited until she'd lain in bed and started reading her book. Then, a few moments after she'd turned off the lights, when she'd closed her eyes and began thinking about all the meaningless tasks she'd need to complete tomorrow, I moved slowly from beneath the bed and reached out and grabbed her ankle. She shrieked. That moment, that single moment, made it all worth it. The rest of the process was sloppy and amateurish: toppling on top of her, fighting off her frantic kicks and swipes, squeezing her neck until her windpipe was crushed, then smashing her head against the wall, just to be sure. I imagine it looked to be the work of a lunatic, not a cunning killer, but the job was done. I'd murdered somebody, and for the life of me, I didn't know why."

Outside, a low groan of thunder and a distant train horn. The mortician pressed the old man's eyes shut, but the eyelids sagged back in their sockets. He placed a small piece of cotton between the lids and the eyes to round them out. Then he worked on sewing his mouth shut, using a curved needle trailed by suture string, passing it through the jaw, under the gums, and back up through the septum.

"You didn't suspect that I'd murdered poor Carol, of that I was sure, but when I helped prepare a body or clean out the retorts I kept waiting for the authorities to enter the mortuary, hands resting on sidearms, and proceed to yank off my fingernails and peel off my skin until I confessed. But despite my carelessness in committing the murder, despite the evidence I'd left behind and the alibi I'd never created, the detectives never came, never even shot me a suspicious glance. Maybe it was because the killer and the killed were both unwanted, nearly invisible. Only a half-dozen people went to her funeral, and that included me..."

Dr. Wagner used an injector gun to freeze Mr. Elliot's mouth. Then he looked up at Kurt and smiled and shook his head. "You're not unwanted, son. Why do you think I allowed your mother to give birth to you? I could have cut you out with a paring knife. Just a small incision above the pubic bone and another in the uterus. Allow a breath and then slit your throat. But, no. I wanted you, son."

Now Dr. Wagner removed a scalpel from his jacket pocket and made an incision near the corpse's clavicle. He scrubbed the vein point clean and inserted a drain tube towards the heart. Kurt assisted by tying a ligature around the lower side of the tube, and then he spoke again.

"After that first murder, I didn't kill for a long time. But whenever I would go out walking, or when I would go to a store, I would pay close attention to the people that interested me—an interest based solely on their generic ordinariness. I followed them and took notes, and eventually I compiled a list of names, complete with occupations and addresses. Michael Robinson, insurance salesman, 2128 Weeping Willow Drive. Suzanne Evans, stay-at-home mother, 4357 Blooming Hills Circle. Tracy Mathewson, hair stylist, 566 Orchard Avenue, apartment 3A. And so on, and so on. I killed them all, Doctor, at first by strangulation and then by scalpel. And now, today, Mr. Elliot."

Dr. Wagner nodded at Kurt and dabbed at his forehead with a handkerchief. With a quick jerk, he flipped on the embalming machine and Kurt watched as the corpse's veins bulged against his skin.

"But you shouldn't be so hard on yourself, young man," Dr. Wagner said.

"Why not? I'm a monster. The Midnight Monster. Why the hell not?"

Several minutes passed and Dr. Wagner didn't answer. Mr. Elliot's body was now fully embalmed and so the mortician turned off the machine. He removed the cannula, tied off the veins and arteries, and worked on suturing the incisions. Kurt stared at his father, and he waited to be comforted, waited... Dr. Wagner grunted and then leaned forward and spoke again.

"Because the world is a hoax, Kurt. A hoax on you and me. A hoax on the dead and the living. And so we have no choice but to play along with the joke. Kill and whore. Booze and torture. But never feel guilt. Never, never, never."

The corpse was smiling and Kurt was sobbing. From the coffin room, they selected a mahogany coffin with praying hands in the interior. The two men picked up the corpse from the preparation table and guided it into the casket. Dr. Wagner had done a nice job on him. He always did a nice job. He gazed at the dead man for a long moment before shutting the casket.

With his slender hands, Dr. Wagner smoothed Kurt's hair and shushed him. "Now stop your crying. The dead can hear more than we think."

CHAPTER 20
THE WOMAN IN BLACK

Detailing his horrific tales had made Kurt exhausted and depressed, so, after spending some time warming his body in the crematorium room, he left the mortuary, got into his beat-up white van (which was used to transport corpses and thus smelled of human rot) and drove through town toward Highway 34. He drove for a few miles, away from the predictability of suburbia, until he came to a long and dark dirt road which led to his little shack in the shadows of the landfill. He parked his van and stepped outside, listened to the coyotes howl and the foxes screech. He limped toward the shack, his ankles deformed from some early violence, unlocked the door, and pushed his way inside. The walls of the shack were covered with clocks, some working, but most not. He was taking after Dr. Wagner in that way, as a collector, and so there were also Teddybears lined on dressers, cabinets, and stuffed in drawers.

He lit a kerosene lamp and hung it on the wall. Then he opened a can of beans and a bottle of beer. He sat at the round table, shoveling the beans into his mouth and washing it down with the beer. When he finished, he remained at the table, staring at his hands. He'd never felt so tired, never felt so lonely.

He took off his clothes and huddled in his sleeping bag. The clocks ticked and the Teddy bears stared. He squeezed his eyes shut and tried to dream pretty dreams, but it was no use because his mind was diseased and he was the Midnight Monster.

Four in the morning and he finally drifted to sleep. But the sleep was restless and terrifying. There were wild grinning faces inside of his skull and they were scratching at his eye sockets trying to get out. He woke and pressed his pillow over his head and then his mouth, trying, perhaps, to suffocate himself. He longed for the dullness of sunlight and soon enough it came.

He arrived back at the mortuary shortly past nine. Inside the preparation room, Dr. Wagner was putting the final cosmetic touches on the corpse and gluing his toupee to his head. Kurt didn't want to startle the mortician, so he stood in the doorway just watching. But Wagner sensed his presence and said: "For in that sleep of death what dreams may come, when we have shuffled off this mortal coil, must give us pause."

Kurt shambled toward the mortician and the corpse. Dr. Wagner was dressed in his Sunday best and so was Mr. Elliot. "Good morning, Kurt," said the mortician. "I hope you had a restful night's sleep. Look at how handsome Mr. Elliot looks. Death has treated him quite well, if I do say so myself. Here are the facts for the day. The viewing will begin at eleven. I am asking that you keep watch over the body. Unfortunately, I have another engagement that I must attend to."

"Another engagement?"

"Something that might excite you as well! A swatch of Clyde Barrow's death pants is being sold at an auction in Ft. Morgan. With the sale of this lovely casket, I just might be able to afford it."

"That's good, sir. I hope you get it. You can't put a value on something like that."

"No. I suppose you can't."

And then, with a practiced somberness, the two of them transported the casket into the viewing area, both of them straining under the heftiness of Mr. Elliot.

"In lieu of a memorial service," Dr. Wagner said, "the viewing will last until five o'clock. Feel free to take a lunch break at one. The register book is inside the register box. Please allow them a few minutes to write a thoughtful inscription before you pull back the curtain. Remember, for friends and family this is not only a time for mourning but a time for healing. And I only pray that you didn't leave any fingerprints or strands of hair at the scene of the crime."

And then, with a strange bow, the mortician left.

The drive-thru idea, of course, had been Dr. Wagner's. This way, people could come by after work or during their lunch break and they wouldn't need to deal with parking or make small talk with people they might have conflict with. They could have a few minutes of private viewing while music played overhead and then they could sign the book, and the victim's family would know that they had paid their respects. If meals could be purchased with such convenience, why not funeral viewings? Eventually, Dr. Wagner joked, they would be able to place a flashing sign that read, "Over one million buried," just like at McDonald's.

The viewing room was tastefully decorated. The wooden casket, with the deceased looking so peaceful, rested on a silver stand. On either side of the room were floor lamps, and surrounding the casket were flowers, discerningly arranged.

But while there was a panel of glass separating him from the mourners, Kurt didn't like being the caretaker of the corpse during viewings. He'd done it on occasion, and most of the time it was hours and hours of boredom, constantly being forced to straighten into a dignified pose when friends and families drove past in the morbid ritual. But worse than the boredom was how those people stared at him, how they studied his albino skin and pale blue eyes. He looked like a monster, he was a monster, and standing next to a lifeless corpse only reinforced that sentiment.

Now Kurt sat on a metal chair and waited. He stared at today's newspaper with its alarming headline: "Will the Midnight Monster Ever Be Caught?" And beneath that, "Forest Grove: A Town Under Siege." But this anonymous notoriety provided little contentment. There was a part of him that wanted to be found out so that his photograph, not just the silly nickname, would be splashed across these same newspapers and magazines and televisions. Of course, he worried about prison. In fact, he was convinced he'd never survive. Behind bars, with such a distinctive face, and with such a brutal history, they'd assault him and rape him and torture him. No, that would never do. When it really came down to it, he was a meek and mild-mannered young man who just happened to have been born the devil.

It was nearly noon when the first mourner arrived. As the funeral music played, the woman took her time writing in the register, providing a message that the dead would never read. Kurt pulled back the curtain and took his place standing stoically behind the coffin. A fat little woman with oversized eyelashes sat in the car gazing at the corpse behind the glass. For several minutes, she studied Mr. Elliot's corpse the way a child would study a monkey in the zoo. Then she took out a camera and snapped several photos. The lighting was good, and the subject never moved. Kurt wondered who the woman was and then decided that he didn't care. She sat there for five minutes or more before the car behind her gave an impatient honk. Without looking back, the fat woman raised her middle finger and then slowly moved forward and drove away.

Next in line was an older woman with gray hair tied in a

bun. She took a quick peek at the corpse and then burst into tears—although the crying fit lasted only a few seconds. She wiped her eyes and nose with a handkerchief, nodded at the albino, and then pressed hard on the gas, skidding away.

Then a man wearing only thermal underwear, and then a family of seven, and then a woman and a man both with oxygen masks. And that's the way it went. Hour after hour Kurt stood in the viewing room, watching over the body, while friends, family, and the curious entered the drive-thru to pay their last respects and thank the Lord that it wasn't them filled with formaldehyde, wasn't them with their mouths sewed shut, wasn't them with their throats slit like sausage casings.

At seven o'clock, the sky turned to soot and Kurt was ready to close up the shop. Dr. Wagner hadn't returned, and Kurt wondered if he'd purchased the bloody pants swath and, if so, which prostitute he was celebrating with and in which cheap motel. With a deep sigh, he closed the lid of the coffin and turned off the lights in the viewing room. Then he returned to his chair and, for some time, sat there in the darkness and the quiet.

He thought of his own illness, thought of his victims gazing at him with those horrified eyes, flopping around like fish, choking on their own blood. The world didn't miss them, indifferent as it was, and since all of their flesh would eventually rot or burn, the cause and time of their demise didn't matter one bit. Throat slit at forty-two or lungs ravaged at ninety-six, death had no memory for the means, no admiration for the fight.

Eventually, he rose from his chair. He realized he was hungry. He would go to the grocery and buy a pastrami sandwich and a Red Delicious apple, and then he would lie in his shotgun shack and dream of the fire.

But he'd only just taken a single step when he heard the crunching of a car pull up in front of the window. Despite the posted hours, despite the darkness behind the glass, the car remained, its engine humming softly.

For some reason, Kurt stopped breathing. He remained in

the middle of the viewing room, paralyzed. Now the engine shut off and the world was quiet. Kurt took a step forward and then another one. What madman was parked outside the mortuary in the dark of the night? He tiptoed around the casket and stood in front of the window. Then he drew open the blinds.

It was a long Lincoln Continental, blue or more likely black. The windows were darkened, so Kurt couldn't see the figure inside. He remained at the window, afraid of his own fear. The figure in the car didn't move.

Why such dread, such terror? Kurt placed his hands on the window and then his face. He stayed like that for another minute or more and then the car window began opening slowly, oh so slowly. But even with the window down, he was having trouble seeing the blackened figure inside. But then the interior lights flashed on, and he saw a woman, a black veil covering her pallid face.

For a long time, Kurt and the strange woman stared at each other, neither of them moving at all. Then the woman reached out a bony hand and pressed the button that opened the register box. She flipped through the pages until she reached the last page. With long and graceful penmanship, she wrote a short message and placed the register back in the box. She returned her gaze to Kurt and a smile spread slowly upon her face. Then she rolled up the window but not before Kurt caught a glimpse of a scarecrow in the backseat, its face blank, its arms missing. The woman drove away slowly, and Kurt watched as the taillights got smaller and smaller until he couldn't see them at all.

The register, the register. With shaking hands, he opened the box and lifted out the thick book. He flipped through the pages, glancing quickly at some of the mournful messages until he arrived at the last page. She had written an address, and beneath the address, four words: "Flesh for the fire."

CHAPTER 21
FOLLOWING ORDERS

He had just left the mortuary and was standing outside fumbling with the lock when he felt somebody grab his shoulder. He gasped and spun around. It was Dr. Wagner, a giant grin plastered on his face. He waved a swatch of bloody cloth in Kurt's face. "I got it!" he said excitedly. "What a prize. Clyde Barrow's death pants. With a signed letter of authenticity. Oh, Kurt. Happiness surrounds me, and I owe it all to you! Just a few more funerals and…"

But Kurt only shook his head brusquely. "I won't be here tomorrow morning," he said. "And not tomorrow night either. I have some people to visit. I have some coffins to sell."

And with that, he left and limped toward his van. Dr. Wagner called after him. "You've done some good in this world, Kurt. Believe me, you have."

"No," Kurt muttered to himself. "Nobody's ever done any good."

That night, Kurt went to the store and bought himself that pastrami sandwich and that Red Delicious apple. He ate the food in his van and then drove through neighborhoods, peering in lighted windows, wondering if there was any possibility for love for a fellow like him, knowing there wasn't.

Once back in his shack, he discovered the heat wasn't working, which wasn't unusual. Exhausted, he gathered as many blankets as he could find and burrowed beneath them. He knew this was the last time he'd be cold, that the fire awaited, and for the first time in a very long time, he had no nightmares.

He woke up with the sun but remained beneath the blankets for some time. And now he couldn't shake the longing for an embrace from the only one who loved him, and it wasn't Dr. Wagner or Reverend Pete or his mother. There was only one.

Two hours later, he stood outside the house that the woman in black had ordered him to visit. It was beige with a long sloping driveway, a three-car garage, a small and tidy lawn, and a single skinny tree. He wore his mortician assistant's suit, only instead of his scalpel, he held the knife that the doctors had given him, the one that was inscribed Cronus. He whispered to the wind, "Mother, I will undertake to do this deed, for I reverence not our father of evil name."

He walked slowly up the pathway, the blade reflecting the blank blue sky and his own translucent skin.

The key was beneath the Welcome mat like he knew it would be. Perhaps, he thought, today would be the day he was caught. Perhaps he would open the door and take a bullet to the stomach, leaving him writhing on the floor, a slug staining the white carpet with blood. That would be an appropriate demise. Just like a slug. But no. He opened the door silently and nobody was waiting for him.

He removed his shoes, his feet still bloodied from the martyr's glass. He moved slowly toward the living room where the sound of a television echoed against the walls. Just in front of the couch, he stopped. A movie was on, a movie he'd seen before: a man and a woman dancing in a field, cheeks pressed against one another. And now they pulled apart for a moment and stared into each other's soulful eyes. The woman. Slender and red-cheeked. "It's now that we love," she said. "Now that we give our hearts to each other and to God."

The man. Strong and square-jawed. "Yes," he said. "A love endless. A love eternal."

And then a long, passionate kiss as the camera pulled away showing the stunning landscape. Sweeping, glorious music played. A love eternal. And then rolled the credits.

So enraptured was he by the movie that Kurt hardly noticed the man and woman sitting on the couch. She wore a white dress and was dabbing at her eyes. She was pretty, and Kurt wondered if she was a heavy bleeder.

Sitting next to her was a burly man with a thick red beard and a long scar on his face. He wore working-class clothes: boots, jeans, and a flannel shirt. He had an enormous wad of tobacco in his mouth and a can of beer between his legs. Unlike the woman, he wasn't sobbing, wasn't making a sound at all. When the woman lay her head on his shoulder, he immediately grabbed her hand and placed it on his crotch. She didn't resist, and that was just like a woman.

Kurt stood there watching them for some time, the Cronus knife dangling from his hand. They didn't know he was there. He took a step forward, the hardwood floor creaking beneath his feet. Both of them spun around in their seats. The woman shrieked, her face revealing an expression of surprise and terror, but the man seemed unaffected. With barely a moment's hesitation, the man reached beneath the pillows of the couch and pulled out a short-barreled rifle. With one thick hand, he whipped the rifle around and pointed it in Kurt's direction. Kurt didn't have time to react. The man squeezed the trigger and there was a loud explosion. Kurt felt a sharp pain as the bullet grazed his shoulder, tearing away flesh. A muted scream, and then he fell to his knees. As he sat there, touching his own blood, he thought that this was it, just a few more breaths, and if he were really honest about things, it was a comforting thought.

The woman was screaming and flailing and pointing, but the bearded man was calm as could be. Without saying a word, he walked around the couch and stood over the bloodied Kurt. With steady hands, he aimed the rifle between the albino's eyes, but this time Kurt was ready and jammed his knife into the man's foot. With an agonized yell, the man dropped his rifle to the ground, and it clattered on the floor. Then, a split second later, he also fell to the floor, collapsing like a marionette.

And now Kurt was the Midnight Monster, and he leapt on top of the bearded-man, pinning his arms down with his knees. Blood was gushing from the man's foot, but still he fought, and when Kurt tried slicing his throat, he used his heft to shove Kurt off of him. Momentarily free, the man crawled toward his gun, and he was screaming in pain, and the woman was screaming in fear, and Kurt stabbed him on the leg once, twice, three times, and then on the back of the neck. The man pulled himself forward like a soldier in the forest, but Kurt grabbed him, flipped him over, and placed the knife on his neck. Then he sliced across, the way he'd done so many times before. The blood spurted everywhere, and the man tried closing the wound with his hands, but soon they were soaked red. Another minute and he was dead, his shirt and pants damp with blood, his hands still on his own neck, his eyes open wide, staring at the devil.

The woman had been watching the whole time, but now she stopped screaming. Maybe her throat was too sore. Instead, she just shook her head, as if her lover were the first man to die a violent death. Kurt wanted to say: What about in medieval England? The drawing and quartering of the non-believers? Or in Babylon: the cutting off of feet, lips, and noses; the blinding and gutting, the tearing out of the heart? Or in Assyria: the skin torn off; a stake hammered through the lubricated anus? And she was shocked by this? By a simple blood-letting?

"Now, now," he said, trying to calm her down. "My name

is Kurt, and I'm just a poor albino boy. Come close to me so I can whisper in your ear, so I can lick your skin."

She was pressed against the wall, her suffering causing her pretty face to become prettier still.

He took a few steps forward and now she made a dash for it, but he knew this house well (had he been here in a dream?) and he cut through the dining room and then the kitchen and nearly caught her at the foot of the stairs. But when he tried grabbing her by the ankle, she was able to kick free. Up the stairs she raced (there was no escape) and she was quicker than he gave her credit. She almost managed to make it to the second floor before Kurt dove forward and got a piece of her leg, causing her to stumble and fall. Her chin hit the top step and she grunted. Panicked, knowing the end was near, she attempted to get back to her feet, but now Kurt had a good grip on her ankle and began pulling her back down the stairs.

"Please," she whispered. "Don't kill me. I won't tell. I won't…"

But that just made Kurt angrier, because he knew that she was lying and that she would tell everybody, and Kurt hated liars and betrayers.

The Cronus knife was in his right hand and he could have slit her throat, just like he did the man, just like he did all of them, but now he felt a hatred so intense that his skin was pulsing and his veins were bulging, and he decided that the blade wasn't good enough for her.

Instead, he swung his right elbow around and connected with her temple, causing snot and saliva and blood to speckle the wall. Then he dragged her up the stairs to the second-floor landing, and she was moaning and pleading, saying, "Please spare me. I'm a good woman. A good daughter. A good wife. Please, please, please, please."

But empathy and kindness had never been his strong suit, so he swung back his leg and kicked her hard in the jaw, knocking a few teeth out at least, then another kick and another and another.

And now was he screaming? Now was he pounding his

chest and jumping up and down like an animal? But that's all he was. An animal. His teeth were sharpened.

He fell upon her, and it was difficult to tell if she was still alive, if her movements were the last moments of consciousness, or only the twitching of post-mortem. He pounded her with his fists over and over again. He hit her so many times, that his own flesh began to tear and meld with hers. He was gasping and shrieking, and he was covered with the residue of another worthless life, another worthless death.

But still it wasn't enough. Not enough pain. Not for her. Not for him. He placed his face against her throat, still pulsing softly, and smelled her just-dead skin, so sweet, like the cedars of Lebanon. The next moment was one of instinct and it was because he was an animal, not a majestic eagle or a proud buffalo, but a cinereous vulture, famished for death. He bit into her throat and chewed her flesh and drank her blood, and then he moved down her body tearing at her breasts and her stomach, swallowing her entrails.

He rose to his feet. The man downstairs was dead, and now so was the woman, her blood dripping down the hardwood floors.

Slowly, deliberately, he walked down the hallway and stepped into the bathroom. He studied himself in the mirror. He didn't look much like an albino now, not with his hair and face and clothes all covered in blood. A smile, and at least his teeth were still white. He turned on the faucet and started washing his hands, scrubbing them really. If he could get his hands clean, that would be something, wouldn't it?

He thought of Dr. Wagner and how happy he'd be that there were two more deaths. Two more bodies to prepare. Two more coffins to fill. It wouldn't be long, any day really, that the old mortician would be able to afford the prized letter from the Zodiac Killer. And wasn't there just as much meaning in collecting serial killer memorabilia as there was in reading the words in the Bible?

He dried his hands on a soft, white towel and dropped the

towel on the ground. Every time he took a step, more blood dripped onto the floor. But none of it mattered. If this was the end of the Midnight Monster, at least, he could say, he'd done it his way.

He was about to head downstairs, about to let Dr. Wagner know he needed to pick out some new pine caskets, when he heard a soft whimper. He turned around. It was coming from the end of the hallway.

A baby.

CHAPTER 22
FATE

Kurt stood in the doorway of the nursery and let his hands fall to his sides. He stared at the twitching and crying lump of flesh in the crib. He thought of all the killings over the years. How many in all? Twelve? Fourteen? He'd lost count. But never a baby.

Breath catching in his throat, he hobbled into the nursery and stood over the crib, his own shadow bending on the wall. The baby's little hands were clenched, his face was purple, and he wouldn't stop wailing. With paternal empathy, Kurt bent down and gently picked the crying little boy out of the crib. He'd never held a baby before. It would be so easy to crush his windpipe, but no. Instead, he just held him. It seemed a miracle to him, but the baby stopped crying almost instantaneously. He pulled the helpless little thing to his chest, shushed in his ear, and bounced slowly, just like he'd seen on television. The baby pressed against him, not knowing the difference between a father and a killer, and Kurt could smell his sweet skin and feel his soft breath and taste his fallen tears. And for the first time in his life, he understood, and he wanted to stay there in that room, holding that little boy forever and ever.

But he couldn't. The walls were covered in blood and

the floors scattered with corpses. He needed to leave. But he wouldn't leave the baby here. He'd take him with him.

If only salvation was a possibility.

If only...

With the baby in his arms (and now the infant's eyes were closed and his thumb was in his mouth), Kurt rushed through the hallway, stepped over the woman's corpse, and stumbled down the stairs. Through the living room where the man's mangled and bloodied body lay ready to decompose, and out the front door, the sun shining brilliantly on God's grotesque creation.

As he walked toward his van, he noticed a woman's face pressed against the window of a neighbor's house, watching him. He thought about entering her house and killing her, too, but decided against it because then he might have to kill her family as well, and then the entire world, and he didn't have time for that.

He drove the transporting van slowly through town, keeping the baby facedown on his lap. From off in the distance, he heard the sound of muted sirens, and he wondered if they were coming for him. He'd done nothing wrong, not really. He was who he was, who he'd been created to be. The baby started crying again, and Kurt rubbed his back and told him to shush.

On the radio, an echo of an old sermon: "But will they ever catch him? This Midnight Monster? He who slaughters the innocent and feasts on their blood? This is what I've heard: he lives in a cave where he has a collection of human skulls of all shapes and sizes, and they are used not for decoration but for sexual gratification. Yes, a monster, a monster, a monster, a monster..."

A monster.

He drove all morning, and into the afternoon. He had no

map, no recollection of ever driving this way, but a force beyond his control was pulling him along, all the while bleeding his soul with a dulled scythe. The highway began angling upward, and the open spaces turned to pine trees and lonesome cabins and jagged rocks. The sun lowered in the sky, and they drove up a winding road, the lodgepoles swaying sinisterly in the breeze. Past abandoned mines and rotted shacks, past piles of carcasses and broken-down cars, until they came to Archer Rock. They were miles from the world, miles from where the baby's sobs would be heard. And now he glanced at the boy, at his face, and realized how much he resembled him. The pale blue eyes. The heart-shaped mouth. The aquiline nose. He would name him Ian and he would be his son.

He parked the van in a little gully and sat there for some time. He wondered if the boy was hungry. It didn't matter. He wouldn't die from starvation. Not from starvation.

A mile, two miles, more, they walked along a blackened river, and every time Ian would start sobbing, Kurt would squeeze him tighter and shush in his ear. And when that didn't work, he would sing a lullaby, his voice not that of a monster but of an angel:

When the bough breaks,
The cradle will fall,
And down will fall baby
Cradle and all.

Now the sun was gone and the sky rolled into infinity. From somewhere the forest animals screamed, and there was no beauty in nature no matter what the writers wrote. The elevation steepened, and Kurt was wheezing badly. "Soon, Ian," he whispered. "Soon."

He was beginning to think that the devil had abandoned him, but then he saw something glimmering beneath a pile of dead leaves. He knew what it was and again he whispered to his son, this time saying, "Fate repeats itself over and over again." He got to his knees and swept away the leaves with his hands. It was a piece of metal, rusted from the elements, the end sharpened into a point. Ahead of him, a dead tree, pulled from the roots.

He held the stake in one hand and the baby in the other. He considered the situation. He wouldn't drive a stake through Ian's feet because he could not yet walk. He was a killer, but not completely unkind. Instead, he placed him in a nest of fallen boughs at the foot of the dead tree. It was a Biblical moment, and Kurt bent down and kissed his forehead. The baby looked up at Kurt with blurry eyes, and his mouth twisted into a little smile. So this is what happiness feels like, Kurt thought. I never knew. Then he whispered, "Goodbye, son. I wish you weren't my son. I wish I wasn't a monster. Then you could live."

And so, the Midnight Monster walked away from the tree, and along the river, and down the mountain, and he never looked back, not once.

CHAPTER 23
ASH AND BONES

When he finally arrived back at the mortuary, it was nighttime, and the moon and stars were shining in a clear black sky. Other than the mortician's black Cadillac, the parking lot was empty. Kurt hobbled slowly toward the front door. Dr. Wagner was waiting for him, wearing his blood-splattered apron.

Kurt nodded brusquely at him. "I see you're still working," he said.

"Yes. But where have you been for so many hours?"

"A woman in black came last night. Faceless scarecrows were in the back seat. She wrote down an address in the registry. I went to the address. I killed everybody."

Dr. Wagner stared at the monster in his midst. But instead of rejecting him like so many before him had, the mortician moved toward him, pulled him close, and embraced him.

"It's an illness," he said. "But illnesses can be cured."

"No. I never had a chance. Not in this world."

"So fatalistic, young Kurt! But certainly it is possible to overcome fate."

Kurt shook his head and said, "I can't overcome fate. I can only be destroyed by it."

"Without you," the old man began. "Without you..."

"Without me, there wouldn't be as much death. That is true. Without me, you wouldn't have as much memorabilia."

The mortician pulled away from the young albino. His eyes narrowed and he stroked his chin. "Which is why I need you, Kurt. Why I need you so very much."

Kurt stared at his own hands. He could feel himself fading. Only a few more words and then…

"As I said, there are more dead. Nobody will miss them. Soon you will be able to buy your letter."

"Yes. I know that is true. I can't thank you enough, but—"

"But in the meantime, I present to you this knife." Kurt reached into his pocket and pulled out the knife, still covered in blood. "As you can see, it has the word Cronus written on it. He was the one who devoured his children, so there might be some symbolism. You can add it to your collection. It will be worth something someday, I think. Considerably more than the Zodiac Killer's final letter."

Dr. Wagner took the knife from his young assistant. His eyes were welling with tears. "You've always been a good boy. I wish things didn't have to end this way. Believe me."

"It ends the same for everybody. I'm no different."

Kurt leaned forward and kissed Dr. Wagner on the cheek. He then turned and walked toward the back of the mortuary, toward the crematorium, while the mortician, fondling the knife between his fingers, watched him go.

Kurt wasn't surprised at all when he saw the woman in black hunched in front of the furnace. Her back was toward Kurt, and she was fumbling with the knobs on the machine. Kurt stood in the doorframe, not saying a word. The woman didn't turn around, but after a few moments she spoke. She had an accent that didn't seem to come from anywhere.

"It's time," she said. "You've lived such a lovely life. But now…"

If he had had more energy, he would have fought her. He

would have made a run for it. But it was too late for all that. He was resigned to his fate. A fate that was never in question. The moment he was cut from his mother's womb, he was destined to be a monster. The moment he took that first breath, he was destined to burn in the fire.

Now the women in black stood on his right. She grabbed his hand. Then she started walking him slowly, deliberately toward the furnace.

"It doesn't hurt," she said. "Just warmth on the skin, is all. Just warmth in the soul."

The woman opened the door. It hadn't been cleaned since the last burning. And who was that? Stanley Maddox's father. Kurt could feel the warmth of the fire. "Do you need help," she said, "getting inside the machine?"

Kurt shook his head, no. "I've been inside many times. To clean the ash and bones."

"Ash and bones," she said.

And even though he said he didn't need help, she lifted him anyway. She lifted him off the ground and into the retort. There was enough room for him to sit cross-legged, as long as his neck was stooped.

He looked out at the world, one last time, and decided he wouldn't miss a thing. The door closed, and a column of flames rose in the chamber. There was no screaming. There was no pounding on the glass. His hair and skin were burned, and then the muscles and soft tissues, and finally the bones, crumbling to the retort floor.

When the cremation was complete, Dr. Wagner gathered the ashes and the bones and placed them in a plain, white urn with the inscription: A Monster Lives Here.

III

STANLEY MADDOX

"How about if I sleep a little bit longer and forget all this nonsense."

—Franz Kafka, *The Metamorphosis*

CHAPTER 24
THE RABBIT RETURNS

Stanley Maddox didn't know where he was. In the middle of the night, all the houses looked the same. Big beige boxes lit by the faint blue glow of the television. Come to think of it, he didn't know exactly why he was wandering through the suburban neighborhoods or how long he'd been wandering. He only knew that with every step he took, his feet ached and burned. Infection was a certainty, gangrene a possibility.

He had vague memories about being chased by a band of pale-faced vigilante doctors, about hiding in a stranger's garage, but that was all he could recall from the previous day. No, that wasn't true. He recalled that he still needed to give his boss, Mr. Elliot, the Sampson loan that he'd worked so hard on. And he was sure that after he gave him the paperwork, after Mr. Elliot understood what a valuable employee he was, Stanley would certainly be hired back full time, with salary and benefits. And how his wife would swoon!

As he walked, he happened to flick his head and got a glimpse of his reflection in a car window. The wound that had spread on his face was completely healed. Or perhaps he'd been mistaken and there had never been a wound in the first place. Things were jumbled in his head and, besides, you can never know about anything for sure.

And now, out of the corner of his eye, he noticed a long, black American car trailing a few feet behind him. When Stanley slowed, so did the car. Furrowing his brow, he picked up his pace and darted toward the next cul-de-sac, but still the car trailed him.

For ten minutes or more, Stanley dodged in and out of the cul-de-sacs and dead ends while the black Buick crept along after him. Finally, he'd had enough. He was infuriated. With a brief infusion of courage, he spun around, shook his fist, and then started pounding on the hood of the car. "What do you want from me?" he shouted. "What do you want?"

He was surprised when, a moment later, the door opened and a man stepped out of the car. With his slicked-back hair, black suit, and white gloves, Stanley recognized him immediately. The mortician from the Drive-Thru Mortuary and Crematorium.

"Dr. Wagner? What are you doing here? Why are you following me?"

"I apologize," the mortician said. "I didn't mean to frighten you. It's simply a marvelous coincidence. I was actually on my way to your house when I spotted you wandering."

"My house? But why?"

Dr. Wagner's mouth twitched and his eyes narrowed. "No reason. No reason at all. But why don't you get in the car? I'll drive you there. It'll save you from wandering aimlessly for the rest of the night."

Stanley thought for a long moment before nodding his head. "Okay," he said. "I thank you. I'm very tired. I don't remember the last time I slept. This will help tremendously."

And so the mortician opened the passenger side door, and Stanley climbed in. He couldn't help but think of that Dickinson poem:

Because I could not stop for Death –
He kindly stopped for me –
The Carriage held but just Ourselves –
And Immortality.

Dr. Wagner followed Stanley into the car and then stared at him for a long moment, his eyes twinkling. "It seems," he said, "that death follows the both of us."

It was a strange thing to say and spoken with no context. The mortician hit the engine, and pressed his foot slowly to the pedal. Handel's Messiah played on the radio.

"My sympathies again about your father," the mortician said.

"Yes. Thank you."

"And do you know when the funeral will be?"

Stanley shook his head. "No. These things are difficult."

"That they are. That they are." A moment's pause. "And what about your wife's service?"

"My wife?"

"But look. We're almost in your neighborhood."

And so they were. Slowly they drove down Meadow Lane and then Sunbird Avenue and then Willow Way. And as they neared his house, Stanley finally noticed the knife that was shining on the dashboard. The knife with the word "Cronus" inscribed on the blade.

"That knife," Stanley said. "Where did you get it?"

Dr. Wagner shrugged his shoulder. "Difficult to say. Perhaps procured from a corpse. Perhaps a gift from my son."

"But it's my knife. I can tell from the inscription. The people at work gave it to me. They gave it to me to celebrate the birth of my first son who we named Ian."

Still driving, the mortician turned toward Stanley which made him nervous. "Of course it's yours," he said. "That's why I brought it along." He then reached forward and grabbed the knife by the blade, gripping it tight enough that it caused his skin to bleed.

He held it in front of Stanley's face, menacingly, before saying, "Take it."

Wide-eyed, Stanley grabbed the weapon, studied it for a moment, and placed it in his lap. "Cronus," he mumbled. "I wonder why they chose that inscription."

"It's probably better," the mortician said, "if we find a place to hide that knife. Just so they don't think that you're the killer…"

"The killer? But that's preposterous. I could never kill. Even if I wanted to. I don't have it in me. It would take a monster to kill."

"And you're not a monster?"

Stanley shook his head. "No. I only work at a mortgage company."

A few minutes later, they parked in front of Stanley's house. Already, there were a half-dozen police cars and ambulances, sirens flashing.

"What happened?" Stanley whispered.

The mortician: "Let's go find out, okay?"

They both stepped out of the car and walked slowly to the house, Stanley in front, Dr. Wagner close behind. A handful of cops stood on the porch, smoking cigarettes, playing dice, and laughing.

When Stanley tried entering, the laughter stopped. "Can I help you with something, pal?" said one of the cops, a baby-faced redhead.

"This is my house," Stanley said.

"Yeah? Well, I wouldn't go in there if I was you."

"Why not?"

"The carnage. Enough to make you vomit. I already did once, and so did Sal." He nodded to his partner standing next to him.

"Please," Dr. Wagner said. "Let the man through."

The officer thought things over for a moment, shrugged, and stepped out of the way. Stanley entered his house, followed closely behind by the mortician.

Inside, more officers were milling about, but it didn't seem that any of them had a real purpose. Stanley took a few steps and glanced around. The living room floor was slicked with blood, and lying near the couch was a man that Stanley recognized as Jeff. He soon became lightheaded and would have toppled to the ground if the mortician hadn't grabbed him and supported him. "Ah, hell," Stanley muttered.

"A knife," one of the officers said. "Probably got him ten, fifteen times. Poor bastard bled to death."

The officers and medics watched as Stanley and Dr. Wagner moved slowly through the living room and toward the staircase. And there on the second-floor landing, Stanley's wife, her face beaten to a pulp, her body bloody and still.

Stanley gasped. "My wife," he said. "My wife."

"Yes. And we should decide on a casket, don't you think? It will be her forever home."

Stanley walked unsteadily up the stairs, grabbing hold of the banister. Then he stood over the corpse, covering his mouth with his hand.

For several minutes he stood there, and then he said, "We got married in early October. I don't remember the day. I don't remember the year. The leaves were beginning to fall. She told me she loved me then. I believed her. Still, one can never be certain."

Dr. Wagner cleared his throat. "May I suggest a solid oak casket with a lilac purple finish? A steal at $2,395. Or, if you'd prefer something more stately, for another five hundred dollars, I could get her into a solid oak casket with a mahogany finish and a cream interior."

"We used to walk along the river, hand in hand. She'd laugh that lilting laugh and we'd talk about our dreams and fears. Did we do that, or am I making it up? Perhaps I saw it in a movie or a commercial. No, I believe it happened."

"Of course, you'll need to decide what type of funeral you'd like. There are so many options. I'd be happy to sit down with you and discuss."

An officer appeared and took several photographs of the corpse. Stanley knew he should feel sad and tried making himself cry, but it was no use: his eyes were dry. Another few minutes with his murdered wife, and then he thought of his son, little Ian. He rose to his feet. "What about the baby?" he asked nobody. "Did anybody check on the boy?"

When nobody responded, Stanley rushed down the hallway with Dr. Wagner calling after him: "Don't forget about an obituary! And flowers! And lunch for the mourners! All of this costs money! But we have payment plans!"

Moments later he stood in the doorway of the nursery. Nobody else was there. Music was playing softly. Brahms's Lullaby. The windows were open, and the curtains were swaying in the breeze. In the corner of the room was Ian's wooden cradle, and it was rocking back and forth, back and forth. Stanley entered the room, having lost so much already. He stood over the cradle and stared at the lump, barely moving, beneath the blanket. With a trembling hand, he lifted back the curtain.

But his son wasn't there.

A rabbit was.

CHAPTER 25
A NEW BEGINNING

Later, they took the bodies away. Dr. Wagner oversold Stanley on a casket and service. It was only money. Nobody helped him clean the carpet or walls, but he didn't mind. Events were easy to forget and the dried blood would help him remember.

That night he had the bed to himself and slept well. The next morning, he returned to Evergreen Lending. He wanted to give Mr. Elliot the Sampson loan, however belated. He owed it to not only Mr. Elliot, but the entire company. He took the elevator to the fourth floor and stepped off. It seemed forever since he'd been at his place of work even though, in reality, it had only been a few days.

Inside the office, he nodded and smiled at a few of the workers that he recognized, but none of them responded. Finally, he arrived at Mr. Elliot's office, but Mr. Elliot's name had been removed from the door and there was a new name in its place: Mr. Gilbert.

Tentatively, Stanley knocked on the door. He heard a muffled voice say, "Come in." He pushed open the door and stepped inside. A man stood at the window, hands clasped behind his back, staring at the parking lot below.

"Excuse me," Stanley said. "I hate to bother you, but…"

The man turned around. He looked to be in his sixties with tightly-cropped gray hair and a handsome, creased face. "Yes?"

"I'm looking for Mr. Elliot. Would you happen to know where he is?"

"Mr. Elliot?" The man shook his head. "No, I'm afraid not. Does he work here?"

"Yes. In fact, this is his office. Although, you've taken his name from the door and replaced it with yours."

"Yes, yes," the man said. "I wonder if he's the fellow who died just the other day. Such a shame. It's the Midnight Monster. He's causing panic throughout the community."

Stanley took a step forward. "At his request, I completed the Sampson loan. I wanted to give it to him."

Mr. Gilbert peered at him over his spectacles. "The Sampson loan you say?"

"Yes, sir. Checked references. Gathered asset documentation. It just needs his signature and…"

The man approached Stanley and grabbed the file from his hand. Licking his fingers, he flipped through the file, nodding his head and mumbling, "Yes, yes. Very impressive indeed."

"I will leave the file with you," Stanley said. "And now I should be going. You see my wife died and my son has gone missing. I'm afraid he's dead, too. Eaten by coyotes, likely."

"A shame. But before you go, I should tell you something."

"Sir?"

"Your work is very impressive. Each i dotted, each t crossed."

Stanley smiled. "I thank you, sir. I worked very hard on it."

"And did you say you were looking for work?"

"Actually, I have a job here as a Mortgage Loan Processor. But my salary has been—"

"But we would be wasting your talents on that low-level job, don't you think?"

"I don't know, sir. I—"

"What would you say to being named our newest Loan Officer?"

Stanley could hardly believe the words coming out of the man's mouth. Not only did a Loan Officer receive a hefty salary, but he was treated with the type of respect that a Loan Processor didn't get.

"It would be an honor, sir. An absolute honor. When would I start?"

A big grin spread across the old man's face. "Is now too soon?"

"No, sir. I'm ready. Absolutely. I'm ready."

"And what did you say your name was?"

"Maddox, sir. Stanley Maddox."

"Wonderful. It's great to have you aboard, Mr. Matthews."

It was a fine day at work. They gave him a new cubicle location, just feet away from the worker's lounge. They gave him a new calculator. A new pad of paper. He worked hard, calling customers and crunching numbers. He didn't remember ever feeling so happy.

At the end of the day, Stanley said goodbye to his colleagues and to his boss, but none of them seemed to remember who he was. That's all right, he told himself. It's better that way.

After work, he was famished, so he decided to try Red Robin again. This time they seated him right away, in a prime corner seat. All around him sat the same people who had been eating at the restaurant the last time he was there. The man and woman with curly red hair were there. The family of towheads. Another family of towheads. And so on and so on.

This time they were all talking about paint. Acrylic and alkyd. Oil and latex. Eggshell and semi-gloss.

"I think," the redheaded woman said, "we should use a

matte sheen. It will soften the glow and mask any scuff marks."

And at another table: "Isn't satin the most durable? Doesn't it have a deep luster?"

Another: "How about Olympic River Reed from Benjamin Moore? A serene blue for total peacefulness."

The waitress came and took Stanley's order. And as he was sitting there, he decided to join in the conversation. Because he belonged. Because he mattered.

"I wonder," he said, his voice cracking, "what sheen and color I should use to cover up the blood?"

Everybody stopped talking and stared at Stanley. He shrugged his shoulders and smiled. A blonde woman cleared her throat and wiped a wisp of hair from her face.

"I would think a matte oil would be your best bet," she said. "It dries beautifully."

The rest of the people nodded in agreement. "Matte oil," they all said.

"Yes," Stanley said. "Matte oil."

A few minutes later his food arrived. The *Whiskey River®️ BBQ* that he'd been waiting so long for. He whispered grace. Then he placed the burger to his mouth, closed his eyes, and took a big bite, enjoying the succulent meat and tangy sauce. But when he opened his eyes, he noticed that everybody was staring at him. A little boy pointed a finger accusingly at him.

With dread, Stanley reached up and touched his cheek. He felt for the flap of skin. And then he started pulling.

ABOUT THE AUTHOR

Jon Bassoff was born in 1974 in New York City and currently lives with his family in a ghost town somewhere in Colorado. His mountain gothic novel, Corrosion, has been translated in French and German and was nominated for the Grand Prix de Litterature Policiere, France's biggest crime fiction award. Three of his novels, Corrosion, The Incurables, and The Disassembled Man have been adapted for the big screen, with The Disassembled Man slated to start filming in 2019 (Emile Hirsch starring). For his day job, Bassoff teaches high school English where he is known by students and faculty alike as the deranged writer guy. He is a connoisseur of tequila, hot sauces, psychobilly music, and flea-bag motels.